JORDIE & JOEY
FELL FROM
THE SKY

JUDI LAUREN

FISH
PRESS
Mendota Heights, Minnesota

First Edition
First Printing, 2022

Book design by Sarah Taplin
Cover design by Sarah Taplin
Cover illustration by Thomas Girard
Back cover: Brush by Brusheezy.com

Jolly Fish Press, an imprint of North Star Editions, Inc.

Library of Congress Cataloging-in-Publication Data (pending)
978-1-63163-581-6

Jolly Fish Press
North Star Editions, Inc.
2297 Waters Drive
Mendota Heights, MN 55120
www.jollyfishpress.com

Printed in Canada

For the alienated and the scarred—
keep believing; the best is yet to come

One-week-old Babies Found in the Middle of Crop Circles

Article written by: Leslie Knowles

Walter Abrams of 2276 Sunset Drive got the surprise of his life when he went out to check on his fields yesterday morning. A portion of his crops had been flattened in a large circle, killing several of them. But more surprising were the twin boys nestled on the outer edges of the largest circle.

"Other than the circle, the field was completely undisturbed. It was like the babies just fell from the sky," Walter, 52, said when asked about the events. "Who leaves babies out in the middle of a field like that? No water, no food, no way to help themselves. Ester and I took 'em in and gave 'em as much as we could, but our babies are long grown and out of the house; we didn't have everything they needed."

The infants, whose names are being withheld, were found with a note, simply stating their names, pinned to their onesies. So far, there's been no progress in tracking down their parents.

"They were very good babies," Ester Abrams, 54, said in her interview. "They barely cried in all the hours we had them. I know it seems unbelievable, but I could tell they were grateful for what we were able to give them, even though it wasn't much. They're beautiful. You can already tell they'll be good people."

The boys are now in the custody of child protective services, and will be placed with a foster family soon. If you have any information on the children or their parents, you're urged to call the CPS Department.

ONE

In the summer of 1947, aliens crash-landed on earth outside of Roswell, New Mexico. I'm pretty sure they were my great-grandparents.

Two

The school door bangs shut behind me and Joey as we enter the building. Like usual, we're running a little late. Mostly because on the way here, Ron Heffley dared my twin brother to eat a dead beetle. Which he did for five bucks.

Now Joey tucks the bill into the zippered part of our shared backpack. Lunch money.

I wait while he stops at the water fountain to drink. A little part of me wants to ask him what the beetle tasted like, but the rest of me is too grossed out to voice the question. He may be only a few minutes older than me, but he's definitely a lot braver. Even if he hadn't had a number one written next to his name on that paper they found on him, I think it's pretty obvious I'm younger.

Joey straightens, wipes his mouth with the sleeve of his green army jacket. Then he nods toward the open classroom door a little ways down the hall. Our homeroom.

Miss Kami is in the doorway, arms crossed over her chest even though her eyes are smiling. "Late again?"

"If the door's not shut, we're not late, right?" Joey asks. He punches my upper arm, then slips into the classroom.

I follow him and take my seat at the desk two down from his. Joey told me that Miss Kami is only nice to us because she feels sorry for us since we don't have a family. I don't really care why she's nice; I only care that school keeps us out of our foster home for eight hours every day. More if we join clubs afterward, but we haven't done that. We don't usually stay in the same school long enough to do that kind of thing.

But that's not the only thing that's great about school.

I check to make sure no one's watching me, then I pull up the search engine on my school-issued tablet. I've been searching for a few months, trying to find anyone who has marks resembling mine and Joey's.

Six circles run down our spines in perfect lines. The circles have circles in them, and then circles in those. In our last school a year ago, one of the guys in the locker room said they looked like crop circles. Everyone at school called us aliens after that.

I think it bothered Joey more than it did me.

Because it sounds weird, but . . . I think it might be true. And if it is true, then that means there's a reason why we don't belong anywhere, why our parents left us when we were babies, and why no one can seem to find them. It explains why no foster family ever wants to keep us.

We just don't belong here. We never will.

At the bottom of my screen, a message icon pops up. Nadia. The girl who sits right next to me in all my classes. I don't really like to make friends because it's always been just me and Joey, but Nadia's not big into taking no for an answer.

She's also not too big into being . . . normal. She carries her books in a briefcase instead of a backpack, and she likes to check people for wires before she talks to them. At first I thought her parents were, like, CIA agents or something, but they're just lawyers.

But I'm not exactly normal either, so it's not like I can judge.

I ignore her message for now. I have limited time on the tablet, and I can talk to Nadia at lunch.

Instead, I focus my attention on the website about UFO experiences. Some of them are a little out there, but I skim them all anyway. If I can find proof that one of the people who've been abducted came back with marks matching mine and Joey's, I might be able to convince him to help me find our birth parents on our own.

Unfortunately, most people who've been on board spaceships only come back with little grooves in their skin, like a piece of them was scooped out. None of them are even close to what we have.

I know they're out there. They have to be. And if I can find them, we'll finally have a family.

THREE

"I messaged you in homeroom." They're the first words out of Nadia's mouth as soon as she's next to me in the lunch line.

"Yeah, sorry, I was researching." I stand on my toes to try and see over the other kids. Joey's still not here, and he has our lunch money in the backpack. English, right before lunch, is the only class I have without my brother. They put him in advanced English.

"Trying to prove you were abducted by aliens again?" Roger Block asks from behind me.

Nadia pushes her glasses up her nose and opens her mouth, most likely to say something nasty about how his parents are divorcing.

"No," I snap at Roger in what is probably the worst comeback ever. But I have to say *something* before Nadia runs her mouth enough to get her into trouble. She's like Joey that way.

Roger laughs, his freckles crinkling along the bridge of his nose.

One of his friends leans up around him. "My cousin goes to Rivercrest and he said you've got marks on your back where they experimented on you. You and your brother."

I shrink back just a little. I'm not like Joey. I'm not brave.

"Show us," Roger orders. "Let's see where the aliens prodded you."

Nadia's hand tightens on her briefcase. Her mouth has turned into a slit.

"Come on." Roger's friend reaches out, grabbing the front of my shirt. He's pulling me closer, like he's really going to tug my shirt up in front of all these people. Just because they don't embarrass me like they do Joey doesn't mean I want everyone to see them.

"Get off him." Joey's voice cuts through the air, even though he pretty much whispered the words. Joey's good at that stuff, at getting people to do what he says.

Roger's friend lets go of me almost immediately. Joey and I've only been going to this school about six weeks, but everyone already knows not to touch me or Joey will do something back. Eating bugs for money isn't the only thing Joey's brave about.

Roger takes a step back. "We were just asking about the aliens."

Joey's face loses some of its color, but I think I'm the only one who can tell. He really hates it when the alien stuff is brought up. I think it's because he's afraid it might be true.

"Stay away from my brother," Joey says. His eyes have filled with anger.

"Whatever. I was done anyway."

I'm not sure why Roger says that. It's pretty obvious to everyone already that he's afraid of Joey.

As soon as Roger's slunk off, Joey turns to me while fishing the five dollars out of the backpack. "Really? The alien stuff again?"

"I'm close," I answer, trying to tell him with my voice that I'm telling the truth. In reality, I'm not all that close. I'm almost certain we're somehow related to the aliens that landed in Roswell, but that's as far as I've gotten. I still can't find anyone with marks like ours. And until I have solid proof, Joey won't go along with it.

Joey hands the bill to the lady behind the counter without taking his eyes off me. He's loaded the tray with my favorites on one side and his on the other. I'm pretty sure the amount on there is worth more than five dollars, but the lady waves us on anyway.

Joey follows Nadia to our usual table by the window that overlooks the red plastic benches outside. It's raining today, so the benches drip with water, which collects in little puddles underneath.

"You should tell the principal Roger's teasing you," Nadia says as soon as I sit next to her.

"Pass," I answer, grabbing the small bag of Ruffles and opening them.

"What you need to do is stop looking up that stuff," Joey cuts in.

Nadia's eyes narrow. "He's not the problem. Roger is. It's not fair for him to pick on Jordie just for being different."

"He won't do it again," Joey answers, shoving French fries in his mouth. He eats like a vacuum cleaner: anything in his area will be sucked down if you're not careful. "He knows I'll break his arm if he does."

"If Jordie just told the principal, you wouldn't have to break anyone's arm."

Joey opens his mouth, but I interrupt. "I'm not talking to anyone, Nadia. And I'll be more careful when I'm looking stuff up, okay, Joey?"

He nods, satisfied.

Nadia huffs and attacks her tuna salad with a plastic spork. I feel a little bad because I know she's just trying to help. But she's lived in the same place all her life, has had the same parents all her life. I'm not sure she understands what it's like when adults really don't care.

Joey meets my eyes from across the table. He doesn't have to speak for me to know what he's saying. That if I wanted to go to the principal, he'd go with me. Or if I wanted him to break Roger's arm anyway, he'd do that too.

Sometimes, I swear I can read his mind. People say it's a twin thing, but I wonder if it's something more than that. Like if it's an alien thing.

I shake my head, letting Joey know I don't want him to do either one. Roger's a jerk, but he didn't actually do anything.

Besides, maybe it is my fault. Maybe I should try to cut back on the weirdness and just be normal. But I don't know how I'm supposed to do that when I can feel how close I am to knowing the truth. And if I manage to find our real parents, people like Roger won't even matter anymore.

Calum's Guide to Extraterrestrials

While Roswell is the most famous location for UFO sightings, it's not the only one. The first recorded UFO sighting was all the way back in 1639, when a guy named James Everell saw a weird light in the sky he couldn't explain. James and the other two guys in the boat with him said that after the light disappeared, they realized they were a mile down the river but had no memory of actually rowing there.

Alien_Boy12:
Are there any records of marks on their bodies after the experience?

Isak:
No, no marks. Honestly, it's never technically been proven that this was a true alien encounter. I mean, realizing you're a mile down the river? Big whoop. I drive all the time and have no memory of getting there.

GreenGirl88:
Ignore Isak, Alien_Boy12. While there aren't any marks recorded, it doesn't mean there weren't any. Remember, in the 1600s, there were so many people being accused of witchcraft. If you were alive back then and suddenly found a weird-looking mark on your body, would you tell someone?

FOUR

I close the tab for Calum's blog with a frown. I do have weird marks, and I'm not interested in showing them to anyone, even in present day. But people losing memories after an alien encounter is something I've heard before. Maybe that explains why I can't remember the first seven years of my life?

"Calling home?" Roger asks, shoving my shoulder with his when he appears behind me.

I ignore him. Joey will be out of the bathroom soon, and I really don't want the first thing he sees when he steps out to be me getting my butt handed to me. That's happened before, unfortunately.

"He can't understand you," Brick—from my English class—says with a snort. "You're not speaking his language."

Roger laughs, then starts making these obnoxious noises, like if all the animals in a zoo started trying to talk to each other.

I turn away from them and stuff the tablet into my locker, where it's supposed to stay when I'm not using it at school.

As I'm shutting the locker door, Roger flicks my ear. It surprises me into jerking, and I end up slamming my finger in the metal door.

Pain shoots through my finger, making me gasp. I pull it out from the door, but the damage has already been done. The skin under my nail is turning purple, and there's a little bit of blood at the edge.

"Aw, hang on." Brick digs in his backpack and pulls out one of those old radios from the '90s. "Here. Try calling your mom."

There's so much glee on his face, I can tell he'd been hanging on to that one for a while. I guess I should give him some credit for that. Brick has trouble hanging on to any thought for longer than a minute.

Unfortunately, instead of forming a comeback, I feel hot tears pricking the corners of my eyes. I can almost understand them poking fun at me for the alien stuff, but there's something about them mentioning calling a mom that hurts more than anything they've said before. Because they *can* call their moms whenever they want.

A blur of blue and green passes on my right, and then Joey's on Roger. The force takes both of them to the ground, and Brick goes with them because Roger reaches out to grab him, as if he can stop my brother.

They hit the floor hard enough to skid, and I hear someone's skin squeak against the tile. The bathroom door is still swinging from where Joey bolted out of it.

"Joey, no." I grab for the back of his army jacket, but the fabric slips through my fingers before I can get a good grip.

He twists, allowing Roger to get on top of him. It's one of his favorite moves. Because it puts the other person at ease, and then he can bring his knee up right where it hurts.

Roger screams, like full-on screaming. He sounds like

Kelly Dobbs when the sixth-grade school iguana got loose in homeroom one day.

Joey pushes Roger off him, then scrambles to his hands and knees, already reaching out for Brick.

"That is enough!" Mr. Robin, one of the hall monitors, storms toward us, breathing so hard his mustache is rippling.

Brick crabwalks backward, trying to get out of my brother's reach.

"Joey, I said that's enough," Mr. Robin repeats.

My brother is feral. His eyes are narrowed and dark. His cheeks have splotches of red on them. His lower lip is swelling from a punch Roger must've gotten in at some point. He grabs Brick's wrist in a punishing grip, but Mr. Robin's had enough.

His large hand closes around the collar of Joey's jacket, and then he hauls him up from the floor. For a second, Joey actually dangles a couple inches off the tile before Mr. Robin drops him down.

The whole thing lasted less than thirty seconds.

"Principal's office. All of you," he growls, pointing. But then he thinks better of it and leads us to the office himself.

Joey and I are semi-familiar with Principal Alex. I get sent here sometimes for daydreaming in my math class, and Joey gets sent here for fighting or for doing something someone dared him to do. We've never been sent here at the same time before.

Brick's still clutching the radio he pulled from his backpack in the hallway. It looks like it got broken in the fight because two of the buttons are dangling off it. It's also making these weird squawking noises. I hope it was expensive.

Roger limps pitifully behind us.

We're a pretty sorry-looking group.

Principal Alex must feel the same way, because he breathes a deep sigh through his nose as soon as we're in his office. It's so powerful I swear it also ripples Mr. Robin's mustache.

"Mr. Robin, please get Nurse Louise," Principal Alex says as he watches Roger collapse into one of the chairs in front of his desk.

Brick's not brave enough to take the other chair. Joey stands behind it and wipes his mouth with his jacket sleeve. A little bit of blood comes off. That's the way Joey always is. I've never seen anyone shrug off pain like he does. He doesn't let anyone else know when he hurts.

"What happened?" Principal Alex asks. Even though his forehead is creased with wrinkles, his voice is soft.

None of us speak. Joey says a black eye is better than being a snitch.

"Boys?" Principal Alex presses.

Brick's gaze shifts uneasily to Roger, but he still stays silent.

Principal Alex sighs again, then says, "I'm sorry, boys. Since no one will tell me, I'll have to call your parents."

FIVE

If Principal Alex was hoping his threat to call our parents would make us squeal, he's wrong. Roger's parents answer immediately, and then they whisk him off to the hospital to make sure he can still have children later in life.

Brick's mom bursts in and drags him out by the ear.

Our foster mom won't pick up the phone. The principal calls three times, and when he can't get an answer, he leaves a message, then tells us we can go home. His voice is soft again when he says that. I think he feels sorry for us the same way Miss Kami does.

As we're getting ready to stand, Principal Alex holds up a hand to make us stop. "Boys, are things bad at your foster home?"

"No." Joey and I speak at the same time. It's not strictly true, but it's not a lie either. Things are rough and uncomfortable there, but they're not bad. We've been in bad homes before. Katie's is nothing like that, even if she prefers we don't speak so she never has to hear us.

"You're sure?" he presses, staring at the both of us. "Because if something's going on, we need to talk about it."

"Nothing's going on," Joey says.

Principal Alex turns his focus on me. He knows I'm the

weaker one of us. His voice goes back to soft. "You've never been in here for fighting before, Jordie."

"He wasn't technically fighting," Joey speaks up before I can respond. "He was standing there while I was fighting. He's just an accessory."

I think he learned that word from Nadia.

Principal Alex sighs, but I don't think it's out of frustration or anger. It sounds more sad than anything. "Look, boys, you're good kids, both of you. If you need help with something, all you have to do is say so."

Joey and I stay silent. We weren't exactly raised to ask for help. Our social worker, Camilla, is really nice and all, but we only see her a few times a year, when she's checking up on us, or when she's switching us to a new home. Other than her, I don't know who we're supposed to ask for help.

Besides, we don't need any right now. Katie's place may not be the best, but we have a room and beds and we're not starving. She also lets us go to school, which a couple of our foster parents didn't let us do. It was why Camilla pulled us from their homes.

"We're okay," Joey says after a long silence. "We don't need any help. I just got into a fight because Roger was being a jerk and making fun of my brother. If anyone needs help, it's him."

Principal Alex closes his eyes and rubs his head. Then he pulls his hands from his face and says, "Okay, you two can go now. I'll see you tomorrow."

We've missed the last bus, so Joey and I walk home. Twice he stops to spit out some blood. I feel bad that he got hit because of me. I shouldn't have let Roger bother me that badly. It's not like he's the first person to ever make fun of me. It'll probably happen lots more times. I can't let Joey get into a fight about it every time. He'll be a mess of broken bones by the time we reach high school.

It's not until we get to Maple Street and the school building is well behind us that I lift my hand to inspect my finger again. The blood's dried around the cuticle, and the skin underneath the nail has turned a darker purple. But at least it's still there.

"He do that?" Joey asks. His voice is angry, like he'd go snap Roger's neck if I tell him he did it.

"No. I mashed it in the locker door." I tuck my hand back in the pocket of my hoodie because the cool air makes the throbbing worse.

We walk in silence for a few more minutes while I work up the courage to say, "I'm sorry about the fight."

"Why're you sorry?" He kicks a pebble and watches it disappear down a storm drain. It rained while we were in school, so I can hear water gurgling down the drain.

"He was teasing me about the alien stuff."

"You can't stop him from being a jerk," Joey says with a shrug. But then he stops and looks at me, staring at me in the way that makes me squirm. "You do know that he'd probably stop if you quit looking stuff about it up online."

"I know." I haven't dared to tell Joey that I've been asking people questions on Calum's blog. Joey would never tease me about that stuff, but I can tell it frustrates him that I keep looking into it.

He grips a lamppost and circles it with his arm extended. "Did you see the look on his face when I kneed him?"

Instantly, an image of Roger's twisted up face enters my mind, and I can't help laughing. It makes Joey smile.

He releases the lamppost and falls back into step with me just as the big blue house at the end of the lane comes into view. Our current foster home.

I take a breath as the familiar heavy dread settles in my stomach. It's not that it's a bad home, but our foster mom, Katie, she doesn't like us to speak. Like ever. She said we're "grating."

Still, we have a couple hours before she gets home at five. It's enough time to make something to eat and disappear into the bedroom we share. We've been doing it this way for the six weeks we've been staying with Katie, and so far, it's been okay.

But today, when we step into the kitchen, Joey says, "We need to pack."

"What?" I turn to look at him with my hand already extended toward the refrigerator. Joey's not usually the person to tell me that. It's almost always our social worker, Camilla. She's been trying to find us a permanent home for years. Every time she shows up to tell us we have to pack, she looks miserable.

"Katie told me that if she got another call from the principal, we were out of here."

My chest tightens. Another foster home? The more we go into, the less chance we'll have of an actual adoption. If we're too much trouble for even foster parents, there's no way anyone will want us permanently.

I squeeze my eyes shut and look away from him so he can't

tell how much the news upsets me. But it's Joey, so of course he already knows.

"Well, what're we going to do? Call Camilla?"

"No." Joey's answer is swift and certain. "We can't do that."

I frown, but keep my eyes shut, like I can block this out if I try hard enough. "Why not?"

Camilla's always been nice to us, even if she hasn't been able to find us a permanent home. I feel kind of bad for her, though. It's not her fault she can't find us one. If we're from aliens, we're never going to fit in with humans.

"They're going to separate us," he says softly.

His words are enough to make me open my eyes. The sun is still shining in through the window over the sink, even though it feels wrong to be so bright outside when we're talking about this.

"What?" I ask, panic pushing its way into my veins. I can't do this without Joey. I've met a lot of kids who hate their siblings, but it's always been just me and Joey. He always has my back like I always have his. I can't lose him.

"You heard me," he answers. "If we call Camilla, then we're going to separate foster homes."

"How do you know that? Did Camilla tell you?"

He shakes his head and looks away from me. "No. She'd written it in our file. I took it to read when we stayed the night at the center waiting to be moved here."

"But it's not our fault Katie doesn't want us." My words come out whiny, like a little kid's. I don't have the energy to be embarrassed about that. We've been over this so many times, in so many different homes. Katie's not the first one to not want us anymore. And she won't be the last.

Unless . . .

"If we're not going to call Camilla, what're we supposed to do?" I wait while Joey's brow furrows, as he tries to come up with an answer. When he stays silent, I say, "I have an idea."

"What?"

"We should go looking for our family, our birth parents."

"Jordie, no."

"Come on." I take a step toward him, trying to get him to look at my eyes even though he's staring stubbornly at the kitchen table. "You already said that we're being separated, so what do we have to lose? Unless you want to be separated."

"Don't be stupid, of course I don't want that." He huffs and crosses his arms over his chest. "I just don't think it's a good plan. You have no idea where to even start looking for them. Besides, Camilla already tried to find them. If she couldn't, with all the connections they have, then there's no way we'll be able to find them on our own."

"Yes, we will. Camilla was looking at human databases."

"Jordie—"

"No, just listen. Please?" I stretch the last word out long, knowing Joey will cave when I do it. He has a look he gives when he really wants me to do something, and I have a tone for it. I just try to be careful with how often I use it, or he'll grow immune to it.

"Fine, I'll listen," Joey says.

"If she's searching human databases, she's not going to

find any matches, because chances are, they're not in any human database. Their DNA probably isn't anywhere close to a human's. They'd be foreign to all the tests and machines and stuff." I start pacing, my feet carrying me around the kitchen because all this energy has to go somewhere. "So we can't count on them ever finding our parents. We have to do it ourselves. I know we can."

Joey hesitates. "But where would we start to look? We were found right here in Payson. Wouldn't you think we were born here too?"

"No, we could've just been dropped off here. Think about it. There are fields with crop circles all over the world. They just land here. They don't stay."

His lips thin out in a line. He's not buying it.

"Don't you want the chance for a family?" It's all I can think about some days. How can it not be on Joey's mind too?

"Fine," Joey relents, but his shoulders stay stiff with tension. "We can go."

I take a breath. This isn't anything I haven't faced before. Joey doesn't believe in this because he doesn't want it to be true. But if I find proof of it, he'll have to accept it.

"I think we should go to the birthplace of alien landings in America."

Joey's turn to take a breath. His arms are tightening across his chest. "Roswell?"

"Yes. If they're anywhere, they'll be there. And if they're not, we can find people who might know where to go to find them. The entire Southwest is full of alien sightings, and we're the area with the most common landings in all of America."

"What if you're wrong?"

"I'm not."

"But what if you are?" His voice turns firm, telling me I have to give him a good enough argument if I actually want to do this.

"Would it really matter?" I ask the big question, the one I know he's thinking of the most. "If I'm wrong, which I'm not, then it doesn't matter. Because we're being split up anyway, so why not try to find our family?"

He shrugs. "Maybe you're right. Maybe we do have someone out there. And if we don't find anything, we can just come back."

I frown. "If they're splitting us up, we can't come back."

Joey looks up at me. "We'll have to live somewhere, Jordie."

Instead of saying anything else, I turn away from him and head into our bedroom to pack the duffel bag we share. We won't come back. We'll find our family and everything will be okay. I know they're out there. And if Joey doesn't think so, then I'll just have to believe enough for the both of us.

SIX

B y the time the air conditioner has coughed itself out, Joey and I have packed our one duffel and backpack with the few outfits we have. I can't believe they're going to split us up. We've managed to stay together in all the foster homes for as long as I can remember.

I can tell Joey really believes it'll happen, or else he wouldn't be doing this. For all the stupid dares he takes, and the fights he gets into, he tries to do his best in our homes. We both know there are only so many foster parents who'll take us both in.

With the money Joey has tucked away, we buy two bus tickets from Payson, Arizona, to Roswell, New Mexico. I don't know where he got the money, but it was most likely earned from bets or dares. Neither one of us is old enough to have an actual job. And it's not like we get an allowance.

Our foster parents are given money to take care of us, but Joey and I don't see that.

After we get the tickets, Joey leads me to one of the black leather seats at the far-left corner of the bus station and tells me to stay put. Then he disappears into the crowd.

I stay on the seat, the backpack in my lap and the strap of the duffel bag clutched tight in my hand, along with my ticket. It feels strange to be doing this. Camilla has always determined where we'll go next. This is the first time Joey and I have decided something big like this on our own.

While my stomach is knotted with fear, there's also a little corner that's starting to wake up with excitement. This is it. We're going to Roswell. We're going to find where we really came from. We're going to learn why we were left in a field, where the marks came from, and if we can get out of the foster system and have a real home.

I also wouldn't mind if we were able to find our real birth date. Apparently, the doctor who checked us out after we were found in the field estimated we were a week old. But no one could find a record of twin boys born who were unaccounted for.

Joey and I count it as the day we were found, and when we lived with a really nice foster couple, they celebrated our ninth birthday with us.

A group of people passes in front of me, and the dark-haired lady at the front of the line gives me a smile. It makes me nervous. I wish Joey would hurry up and get back here. Our bus is supposed to leave in thirty minutes.

My stomach dips as I start to imagine that maybe Katie came home early and found out we left. Maybe she called Camilla and they're looking for us. If they get us back, they'll definitely split us up. One of us is way less trouble for a foster parent than the both of us.

Before my panic can make its way through my entire bloodstream, I see Joey coming back. His shoulders are tense, but he walks with ease. When we left the house, he'd washed the blood off his face, so no one's staring at him.

"Where were you?" I hiss as soon as he sits next to me, nudging the duffel bag with his sneaker.

"The bathroom," he answers. "You should go before we get on the bus."

"I don't have to go."

"That Gatorade you had at lunch not doing anything?"

As soon as he says that, I feel the need to pee. But I don't want to give Joey the satisfaction, so I keep sitting there.

Again with his alien mind reading, he smirks. Then he pulls his math book from our backpack and starts doing our homework.

"What're you doing?" I ask, wincing as my voice cracks.

"Homework," he answers without looking up.

"Why? When we find our family in Roswell, we won't have to come back here."

His lips press into a line, but he doesn't speak. He doesn't have to. I get it. Even though he's coming with me to Roswell, he doesn't believe we'll actually find anything there.

"Why're you doing this?" I demand, my neck heating. "If you don't think there's anything there for us, why're we going?"

"Because maybe I'm wrong," he says. "And besides, anything's better than being split up." He looks up suddenly, searching my face. "Right?"

"Of course."

He nods and goes back to the math book. I don't bother with homework. I *know* we're going to find our family in

Roswell. We'll find people with marks like ours, and we'll have a family. And when the proof is right in front of his face, Joey won't be able to deny it.

Calum's Guide to Extraterrestrials

The first widely publicized alien abduction was Betty and Barney Hill of Portsmouth, New Jersey. It's also known as the Zeta Reticuli Incident since the Hills said they were abducted by aliens who were from the Zeta Reticuli system. South of Lancaster, on US Route 3, the Hills saw a bright light that appeared to be moving upward. While the Hills were still in their car, the UFO flew above them and abducted them from the vehicle. The Hills lost consciousness, and when they awoke, they discovered they were thirty-five miles past the last point they remembered. The strap on their binoculars was torn, Betty's dress was ripped, and the toes of Barney's dress shoes were scuffed.

Ten days after the abduction, Betty had vivid dreams for five nights of what happened to them aboard the ship. While they had no physical marks on them, Betty remembered a needle being driven into her navel.

Betty and Barney's abduction was the first real proof that aliens are testing humans. But the reason why remains a mystery.

Alien_Boy12:
Is it possible the aliens are looking for someone specific?

Calum:

It's highly possible. Because the abductions are spread over so many areas, it stands to reason that they're testing humanity as a whole. However, I don't think the extraterrestrials are as clinical as most would have you believe. I think it's probable one (or more) of them actually does walk among us, and that's who they're looking for.

SEVEN

When I get out of the bathroom and go back to my seat with Joey, I find it's occupied. By Nadia. Her briefcase sits at her feet, the toes of her black Mary Janes pressed to the handle.

"What're you doing here?" I ask before I can stop myself.

"Your brother called me," she answers. "He really is the smart one."

My gaze moves to the suitcase sitting next to her briefcase, and my stomach jumps. "You're not coming with us."

"Of course I am." She adjusts her glasses. "Joey told me about the state thinking of splitting you up. On the drive to New Mexico, I'm going to try to find something that says the two of you can't be split up."

I cross my arms over my chest. "Why can't we just ask one of your parents? Wouldn't they know?"

"Sure. But if you want legal counsel from them, they charge way more than you can afford. Hundreds of dollars an hour." She pushes her briefcase with the toe of her shoe so it wobbles. "I, on the other hand, can be bought with cheeseburgers."

I glare at Joey, and he glares back. After all this time he's told me to try and keep the alien thing low profile, he's inviting Nadia with us? As allies go, she's not a bad one. She's wicked smart and is pretty nice once you get to know her. But I don't want her along. If we really do manage to find a family in Roswell, how will we explain that to her? Her parents are lawyers. I'm pretty sure to be one of those, you can't believe in things like UFOs.

"Don't be mad at each other," Nadia says without looking at either one of us. She has a ticket that matches mine and Joey's clutched in her fist. "It's not logical to be angry about this. Joey's right, Jordie. You two need help. Isn't it more important that you two stay together than anything else?"

Some of the fight leaks out of my body like a balloon being squashed. That is more important, at least to me. Joey's been with me through everything. Even if I can't really remember the first seven years of my life, I know Joey was there. We came into the world at almost the same time. We survived hours alone in a field when we were just babies. And before that, we spent nine months growing. If that's how long alien babies take to grow. I'll have to see if Calum's blog has any information about that.

"Fine," I say. "You're right."

"I know." She smiles when she says it, like she's letting me know she's not trying to be a know-it-all. It doesn't really help. It's a good thing she actually is smart.

The clock above the desk clicks over to five p.m., and Joey says, "It's time, guys."

He grabs the duffel, so I grab the backpack, and then Nadia's suitcase. It's heavier than I thought. She watches me heave it for a few minutes, then shows me how to pop the handle so I can use the wheels on the bottom.

We go through the line, then hand over our tickets. Joey

keeps checking behind us, like he's worried Katie or Camilla will find out where we are and track us down.

My own muscles are locked. Sweat has broken out on my forehead.

The brakes squeal on the bus as the doors close. Even as I watch the bus station disappear behind us, I still don't relax until we're out on the highway. In a little under two hours, we'll stop to change buses in Phoenix. We're stopping again before we reach Roswell, but I'm not sure where.

But the cities in between don't matter. Roswell is where we need to be. And more than that, Calum is based in Roswell. He travels all over for his blog, but he spends most of his time in New Mexico.

I already messaged Calum privately to see if he would be willing to meet with me once I get to Roswell. I haven't told Joey. He's coming with me only because it means we might not be split up, but he doesn't believe. And if he doesn't, then I don't want him meeting Calum.

I know it's not an incredibly smart idea to meet someone from the internet that I don't actually know, but I don't have a choice. I'll have to be careful. At least we're meeting somewhere public.

For now, I settle back in my seat. We managed to get seats together, so I'm between Joey and Nadia. I'm still irritated that he brought her along, but at least we're gone. At least we're still together for now.

Nadia takes a small laptop out of her briefcase and opens

it up on her knees. "So how many homes have you guys been in total?"

"Nineteen," Joey answers immediately, while heat creeps into my cheeks. Joey doesn't mind the number of homes we've been in, or the fact that we can't seem to find anyone who wants to keep us. He says it's the way life is.

I don't understand how he does it.

"What were the reasons for why you were moved out of all of them?"

"Why do you assume it's our fault?" I snap.

Her eyebrows rise above her glasses. "I didn't. I was simply asking."

"It's okay," Joey says, giving me a look. The one that says I need to knock it off or he'll put me in a headlock. Even though we're the same height, he's a lot stronger than me. He can pin almost anyone; I have trouble making sure our backpack doesn't drag me down when I wear it.

I shift my gaze out the window so I don't have to see him. I don't want to have to hear all the ways we failed foster parents over our short, miserable lives.

Joey tells her all of it. He starts with the good ones. Darla and Mitch, who had us for eight months—the longest home we had—before Darla was diagnosed with cancer. They didn't think two ten-year-olds should be around that kind of thing. There was Malia and Chad, who took us in when they thought they couldn't have kids, but then Malia got pregnant with triplets. Those were two of my favorite homes.

But then there was the family whose house burned down a

few weeks after they took us in, the old couple who didn't like us to speak, the foster dad who made us stay home and work instead of go to school.

Then there are the other ones. The foster mom who kicked us out after Joey got into one too many fights. He was usually defending me, but not always. I think sometimes Joey just likes to fight.

Then there was the couple who gave us back when their toy poodle "didn't like us," the couple whose grandchildren didn't want us around. There was a foster dad who wouldn't feed us, and another one who used us to steal laptops and sell them before he was busted.

Nadia nods along with every story, stopping occasionally to ask us a question. Then she says, "We're missing one. What happened in the one you were in before you moved in with Katie?"

"Oh." Joey laughs, low enough that no one looks over at us. "He caught me in the middle of a dare. His real son had dared me to kiss him for ten bucks, so I did. His dad caught us and was pissed. Then Camilla put us with Katie."

I don't correct his story. I was at the kitchen table when it happened, in full view of the living room, but I don't think they realized I was there. The boy, Carl, hadn't dared Joey. And there was no money. I think it was just something they wanted to do.

Nadia makes a final note, then frowns at her computer screen. "There have to be more people in Payson willing to foster twins."

"Maybe Henry the computer thief will take us back in when he gets out of prison," Joey says.

My lips pull up in a smile even though I don't want them to. It was actually not bad at Henry's place. Sure, he was a thief and a gambler, but he was a nice guy. He packed lunches for us and made sure we had a few bucks in case of an emergency. Even though I knew stealing the laptops was wrong, I never told anyone, and neither did Joey. It was a good home.

Nadia sniffs in clear disagreement. "I'm pretty sure you can't have a criminal record if you want to foster kids."

Oh. I hadn't even thought of that. How many people in Payson have a criminal record?

"You also have to have the right-sized home," Nadia continues. "If it's deemed too small, you can't foster. Income is also a factor. You have to be financially stable to foster."

"Henry was financially stable," Joey points out.

Nadia huffs and pulls her glasses off to clean them on her dress shirt. Yeah, she's wearing one of those.

"If you want real help, you should stop making jokes."

"Okay," Joey says. "Sorry."

She puts her glasses back on, pushes them up on her nose, then puts her fingers back on the keyboard. "So it looks like the majority of the homes you've been in, the reasons why you couldn't stay weren't your fault."

I cut her a glare.

She ignores me as she reads over the notes. "It seems like you guys had to leave just because."

"What did you expect?" I ask, my temper heating like the

Arizona sun beating down on the top of the bus. "Since we've been bounced around so many times, you thought we must've done something to cause it?"

"I never said that." Red splotches appear on her cheeks.

"It's what you were looking for."

"I was asking for facts!" Her voice rises enough for a few passengers to turn and look at us. I shrink a little in my seat. Being noticed is Joey's thing. I'd rather not.

Nadia takes a breath, then shuts her laptop. "I'm going to that empty seat near the front. I need to work where I won't be interrupted. Joey, I'll come back if I have any questions."

She jostles my knees with hers as she moves because I won't pull my legs back. In a rare swap of personalities, Joey scrunches his legs up so she can get out easily.

As soon as she's gone, he looks at me. But it's not the same look from before, the one where I know I'm going too far. This time there's a little bit of pity in his eyes that makes me squirm.

"Did you hear her questions?" I ask.

"Yeah. I didn't like them either. But she doesn't know us, Jordie. She's just trying to get everything. And she's helping us just to be nice, you know. She's buying her own food, not asking for payment in burgers."

I set my shoes against the empty seat in front of me and push. "She looks at us like other people do."

"How do other people look at us?"

"Like there's something wrong with us just because we don't have a family." I swallow because my throat's starting to feel tight. "Maybe . . . maybe there is. Why else would our parents leave us in the middle of a field?"

"It's not you," Joey says firmly. "And since I'm the other half of you, it's not me either. There has to be an explanation, and we'll find it. Just because I don't think the answer is aliens doesn't mean that it isn't. You could be right. And if you are, I promise I'll never make you stop saying 'I told you so.'"

That gets a smile out of me. Joey's always good at that, at calming me. I like to think I can do the same for him, like we're one planet in our own little galaxy.

EIGHT

When we reach Phoenix, Nadia's acknowledging my existence again. Just barely. But that's okay, because I'm barely acknowledging hers.

Joey walks between us as we get off the bus, acting oblivious to the fact that Nadia and I are communicating by glares. But most people underestimate how much Joey and I actually notice. When people would rather pretend you don't exist, they tend to forget you still watch them.

"We have an hour and fifteen minutes before the bus leaves for Las Cruces," Joey says, checking the time on his watch. "Let's get something to eat."

We wander around for a few minutes as the sun sets. Then Joey points out a diner with a giant coffee cup on the roof that has a big chunk of green spilling out of it, like radioactive coffee. Mel's Diner.

"Come on," Joey says, tugging on my sleeve.

Nadia and I follow him across the parking lot and into the building. The floor is this old black-and-white tile that makes me dizzy to stare at for too long. One side of the diner has a long counter with gray chairs lined up. The other side has several booths and rectangular tables.

Joey leads us to one of the tables and slides into a booth.

I follow him, and Nadia takes the seat across from us, setting her briefcase down carefully in the empty space beside her.

"So?" Joey asks. "Did you find anything out?"

"I'm still working on it," she admits, her nose scrunching like she hates that she doesn't have an actual answer yet. "How long has Camilla been your caseworker?"

I look at Joey to find him watching me. "Since always, I think? I don't remember another one."

"Yeah, it's always been Camilla," Joey says.

From her slow nod, I'm guessing that's not good news. "Is she nice to you guys?"

"Yes," Joey answers immediately. "She's really nice."

"So you don't think she's splitting you up because she wants to?"

"What reason would she have for that?" I ask.

Before Nadia can answer, a waitress appears at our table, a pad and pen in her hand. She gives us all a big smile. "What can I get for you three today?"

We all order burgers and fries, and I order a Coke while Joey and Nadia ask for milkshakes.

As soon as she leaves in a cloud of flowery perfume, I look back at Nadia. "Well? What reason would she have?"

"I don't know." She shrugs and tucks her menu back behind the napkin dispenser. "That's why I was asking."

"A lot of people are willing to foster a kid, but not two," Joey says, his shoulders dropping enough that I'm not the only one to notice.

"We'll figure it out," Nadia replies, trying to make her voice sound more upbeat. "There has to be something. Something that can prove you two have to stay together. Do you guys have any health problems?"

I shake my head. The marks on our spines weren't caused from anything, and we're mostly healthy, which I've always been grateful for. It's hard enough getting moved around from home to home.

Nadia chews on her lower lip as she stares out the window. She doesn't move, not even when the waitress comes back with our food. Joey and I start immediately, and I burn the tips of my fingers on the steaming French fries.

"There has to be something," Nadia says with a decisive nod, like she can make it so just by speaking it out loud. "I'll find it, guys. I promise."

Calum:

It's great to hear from you, Alien_Boy12, and I'm glad you reached out! Yes, I will be in Roswell tomorrow. I'm actually meeting up with a few friends of mine at the Cowboy Café at noon for lunch. You're welcome to come. We'd be more than happy to talk to you about everything we know about Roswell and the UFOs that've been in our city for decades.

NINE

I feel better after reading the private message from Calum on Nadia's phone. If anyone will be able to tell me about Roswell and where the aliens might be, and if we could be related in some way, it's Calum.

And maybe if I can talk to someone who believes in that, I can get Joey to at least consider the idea that it's real. Nadia, on the other hand . . .

When we board the bus headed to Las Cruces, Joey takes the middle seat this time. I feel a little bad about the way I talked to Nadia because she's doing this just to be nice, but talking about the different homes, the fact that we've never managed to get anyone to like us enough to keep us, makes my stomach hurt.

I don't see how Joey can talk about it like it's no big deal.

Nadia opens her laptop, balances it on her knees again, and goes back to typing. The bus is dark, so the light from her screen reflects in the lenses of her glasses.

Joey leans back in his seat, stretching his legs out and yawning. I guess I should probably try to get some sleep, but I don't think I could turn my mind off for that. I *have* to find something in Roswell, something that can help us find our family. If I don't, Joey and I will end up back in Payson and separated.

I look at him from the corner of my eye. His head's leaned

back and his eyes are closed. For all the time Joey and I have spent crammed together in rooms, or even in closets, he never irritated me enough for me to wish he wasn't there.

I hope he can say the same about me.

If they're going to separate us, there's no way I can go back to Payson. I can't lose Joey.

"It'll be okay, Jordie," Nadia says suddenly, so softly I wonder if I was actually meant to hear her.

I look over at her. The streetlights zipping by outside cast weird yellow glows over us every few seconds. It's like the world is taking picture after picture of us. "If you can't find anything, we can't go back to Payson."

"Where will you go?"

"I don't know." I haven't thought that far ahead.

Three more streetlights pass outside. Then she says, "Running away won't solve anything, you know."

I flick my gaze to Joey, where he sleeps right next to me. "We're not supposed to be apart, Nadia. We're twins. We weren't meant to be separated."

She nods like it was an answer to a question, then goes back to typing on her laptop.

I go back to staring at the seat in front of me. Roswell's still about nine hours away. If we stay on schedule, we should get there around seven in the morning. Plenty of time to meet up with Calum at the café.

"What exactly are you planning on doing when we get to Roswell?" Nadia asks in a whisper.

"We're just looking."

"No, I know that. I mean, where? Roswell is huge." She looks away from her computer and frowns as Joey snores.

I consider telling her about the alien thing, but I'm worried Joey won't like it. And since both her parents are lawyers and Nadia only deals in facts, I'm not sure she'd believe in aliens.

"We're just looking," I finally say, watching her phone light up with a message from her dad. "He doesn't care you're coming with us?"

"They're away at a conference and won't be home until this weekend. They had a nanny staying with me, but I convinced her Mom and Dad had come back early." She shrugs with her eyes still on her laptop.

"Do they go away a lot?"

"Yeah, but not usually at the same time. They like to make sure I'm not alone." She glances up suddenly. "I don't *need* a nanny. That's just so Mom and Dad don't worry about me the entire time they're gone."

I nod as if I understand what that's like. I don't know how it feels to have a mom or a dad, let alone one that would worry enough about me to have someone stay with me.

Nadia seems to realize where my mind's headed because she clears her throat and goes back to her laptop. "I do wish my parents had reproduced more. I would like to have a brother or sister."

I close my eyes. "You talk so weird sometimes."

She chuckles. "So I've been told. You can go to sleep. I'll wake you if I find anything that might help."

I hope that we won't need it, that we'll reach Roswell and

find our parents, or at least a hint of where they are. Because if we can't find anything in New Mexico, it won't matter what she discovers.

TEN

The white light blinds me. I'm so hot all over. It feels like my skin is on fire. I raise my hands, trying to scratch it off.

"Shh." Someone leans over me, the head so large it blocks the bright light. "You're okay, Jordie."

I close my eyes again because even with her blocking out the light, it still hurts to look at it. Everything hurts. "Mom?"

The woman squeezes my hand in response. It's her.

"We have to get them to safety," she says, her voice full of command and urgency.

I try to open my eyes, to get a better look at her, but the lights are starting to spin in a circle. They're different colors now, blue and green. The floor's moving.

Long, rubbery fingers grip my wrist.

"We have to send him now," the woman says. "He needs to go."

I jerk awake with a start when something pinches my arm. My lungs ache, so I draw in a breath, trying to remember where I am. This isn't the room I share with Joey at Katie's house. This is . . .

"Come on," Joey says, poking my arm again. "The bus is stopped. We got to wait a couple hours for the bus to Roswell to leave."

I grab our backpack and stumble up from the seat. Joey

takes the duffel bag. My palms are sweaty and my heart's hopping around like a rabbit. I've never dreamed about my mom before.

When we step off the bus and into the cool New Mexico air, I shut my eyes, trying to hang on to the images I saw. But they're just flashes. The lights, my mom, the feeling of the ground spinning underneath me. I've never felt movement like that, like we were going hundreds of miles per hour.

I open my eyes and follow Joey and Nadia across the parking lot and into the bus station building. The colors around me feel too bright, the people too loud. I focus on the back of Nadia's head so I don't lose her in the crowd. I'm not worried about losing Joey. We always find each other.

I can't believe I dreamed about my mom. I heard her voice. That must've been right before we were left in the field. It had to be. No woman has ever come forward to claim us. So the only time I could've heard her talking was when we were still with her. And the lights and the speed . . . We had to have been aboard a spaceship.

"Dude." Joey grips the back of my T-shirt suddenly, jerking me to a halt. I look up in time to see my hand on the door to the girl's bathroom. The door Nadia just disappeared into.

"I know you like her, but that's a little much," Joey says, tugging on my shirt to get me to turn into the other bathroom.

"I don't like her," I huff, shrugging free from his grip.

"Relax," he says. "We keep each other's secrets."

We use the bathroom and I stand against the wall while Joey splashes water on his face. His eyes are bloodshot from his interrupted sleep, and his cheek has a line on it where he must've pressed it into the headrest on his seat on the bus.

"Do you ever dream about Mom?" I ask, my voice loud in the nearly empty bathroom.

"You mean dream about what she's like?"

"No, like memories of her."

"Oh." He grabs a paper towel and presses it to his face. "No. But they found us in the field when we were like a week old, Jordie. I doubt either one of us has actual memories of her."

I track a line of grime down the wall with my gaze. "I think we do. Even if we were that young, we still technically have the memory. We lived it."

He crushes the paper towel in his fist and looks up at me. "Where's this coming from? Did you remember something?"

I hesitate. I doubt Joey will believe me, but we tell each other everything. It's how we work. "Yeah. I had a dream about her."

"How do you know it was her?"

"I asked her."

"And she said she was our mom?"

"Well . . . not with words." I remember the way she squeezed my hand, so tightly. Like I mattered. "But it was her."

He tosses the paper towel in the trash bin. "I don't know. I mean, I guess you have a point about the memories being there, even if we were young. But it's a little . . . coincidental that you started dreaming about her on our way here. Don't you think you could've done that because you've been thinking about her so much over the last couple days?"

"No," I say flatly. "I'm telling you, Joey, it was an actual memory. It wasn't something my mind made up. You promised you would be open to the idea of Roswell."

He holds his hands up. "You're right. Okay. Maybe it is a memory." I can tell from his voice that he still doesn't truly believe it could be one. He lowers his hands and stares at them. Then he says so, so quietly, "We need to talk about what we're going to do if we don't find anything in Roswell."

"No, we don't." My heart squeezes so tight in my chest it's like I can't breathe. "We'll find it in Roswell. We'll find our family."

"But—"

"We will," I say, raising my voice over his. Heat is spreading over my cheeks.

"Okay," he says with a nod. "I'll be outside."

He disappears, the door squeaking shut behind him before I have the chance to say anything else.

I take a breath, trying to get that squeezing in my chest to go away. Bracing my hands on the cool porcelain sink, I stare at my reflection in the mirror. Identical to Joey but so different from him.

He doesn't understand. It can't be just a dream. It has to be a memory, coming out now because we're so close to finding our parents, our family. It can't be anything else.

ELEVEN

We spend the hours waiting for the bus to Roswell in the bus station. It's almost three in the morning at that point, so it's not like we have a lot of options anyway. Joey finds a set of chairs that's missing an armrest between them so one of us can lie down. Nadia didn't get any sleep on the bus, so she takes it. After leaving us detailed instructions of how to keep watch over her briefcase.

She may as well have handcuffed it to my wrist.

Joey sits next to me in one of the hard chairs, his legs stretched out in front of him. His eyes have that faraway look they always get when he wants some space to move in. Twice I watch him eye the automatic doors at the front of the bus station.

"You can go for a walk if you want," I say. Nadia left her phone with us, so we've been taking turns playing a cooking game on it. Hopefully we'll be well separated when she realizes we bought the app through her account.

"I don't know." Joey hesitates, sending another longing glance at the doors.

"Go ahead. I'm fine on my own. You know that."

His leg is starting to bounce from all the unused energy. "Sure?"

"Yeah."

He stands and heads for the doors, but he looks back at me, like he's still unsure. I wave him on. It's not like Joey and I have never been separated before. We've both been on different sports teams and had different classes in school. And it's not like he's walking to Texas.

So I settle back into the game, pressing my back into the lumpy chair to try and keep myself awake. The nap I took on the bus seems like it happened a year ago.

A man in a blue hoodie passes by me so close I have to pull my legs back so he doesn't trip over them. I glance up to give him the look I've seen Joey flash people, but his hood's pulled over his face so I can't see him.

As soon as he passes, I look back at the phone. Nadia's background is a picture of her toy poodle Mittens. Joey and I stayed at a house with a huge dog once. It terrorized Joey from the day we got there until the day we left. Henry the computer thief had a dog too, a cocker spaniel that went to Henry's brother when Henry was arrested. Joey and I both want a dog, but we know it can't happen until we get a permanent home. Maybe when we find our parents we can get one.

Glancing up once to make sure Nadia's still sleeping, I click on her photo gallery. There are tons more pictures of Mittens, and then pictures of her and her parents. I stare at their faces, at the smiles and the tan lines and the brightness.

I can see Nadia in both of her parents. Her dad's ears, her mom's nose. The way they lean into each other. Nadia even has a freckle on her shoulder that matches one on her mom's.

Even though I look like Joey, I want others who look and talk like me. I want parents. I want a family.

My mind flashes back to the dream I had of my mom on the bus. Except . . . it didn't feel like a dream. No matter what Joey believes, it was a memory. And I think she sent it to me on purpose. We're getting closer to Roswell; we have to be getting closer to her. Maybe closer to our dad, our whole family.

Calum said on his blog that Betty Hill had vivid dreams, memories, for five nights after they were on the UFO, but it wasn't right after. Maybe there's something there, something that could explain why the memories are happening now instead of years earlier. Maybe I did have them earlier and just can't remember?

I glance up, checking again that Nadia's sleeping. Her glasses have slipped a little down her nose, and her mouth's hanging open. She looks very different sleeping than she does awake.

I wonder what her parents would think if they knew what she was doing, if they knew that she'd snuck out to go to New Mexico with some kids from her school that she barely knows. She'd shrugged when she said she hadn't told them, but I'm guessing since she didn't let them know about it, it means they would care a lot.

Henry was the only one of our foster parents who cared about stuff like that. He was the only foster parent we lived with who was a thief, but his home was also one of the only ones where I felt truly safe.

But what does that say about us? That the only one who

could stand to be around us that long was a man who didn't even follow the law and is now serving eight years in a state prison?

I drop my gaze back to Nadia's phone and go to Calum's blog. Then I search his archives to see if this is just another thing that separates me from the rest of the world.

Calum's Guide to Extraterrestrials

In March 1997, thousands of people in Arizona witnessed a phenomenon that remains unexplained. Through a 300-mile stretch of land from Phoenix to the Mexican border, people saw weird lights from around seven to eleven p.m. flying in a V formation. It's reported to have been the length of several football fields.

All the lights were red, except for a single white one at the tip of the V. Witnesses stated that the aircraft seemed to have no engines and made no noise. Governor Fife Symington witnessed the formation as well. At the time, he stated they weren't aliens. However, after he retired, he said the lights and machines were definitely not made by humans. Perhaps if he hadn't felt pressured to lie about what he'd witnessed, we'd be a lot further in knowing what happened that night.

Unfortunately, that's an all-too-common occurrence when it comes to witnessing UFOs or aliens. Those who don't believe have a tendency to make a mockery of abductees or witnesses. They can be bullied in school and online, and even in the workplace. It's why the term "alienated" is so on point and specific to these cases.

Any experiences with extraterrestrials will make you differ-ent from everyone else on earth. Only those who have been abducted or witnessed UFOs can truly understand how you feel. While I was never abducted, I did live with someone who was. Believing them is the first step to helping them heal.

Twelve

Joey comes back into the station about fifteen minutes before the bus is supposed to leave for Roswell. His hair is shoved back from his forehead; his steps are lighter as he makes his way toward me. But then they falter, and he meets me with a frown. "Where's the backpack?"

"What?" I click out of the window I had open of Calum's blog and glance down at the floor, where the backpack should be propped up next to our duffel bag. But it's gone. So is the duffel bag. The only thing left is Nadia's suitcase, which only has her clothes in it. Even her briefcase is missing.

"What happened to our stuff?" Joey demands. "I told you to keep an eye on it."

"I was. I did." The words stick in my throat. "I-I don't know what happened."

"Someone took it," Joey snaps. "It's obvious what happened. How could you do something so stupid? You said you would be fine if I left you alone."

I shrink a little into my chair, my cheeks heating. "I'm sorry."

Nadia sits up on the bench across from me, rubbing her eyes and yawning. "What's going on?"

"Jordie lost our stuff," Joey says. "Including your briefcase."

"What?" She shoots up from her spot and starts searching

the floor, as if one of us somehow missed it. When she realizes it's not there, she looks up at me with so much betrayal in her eyes that my stomach lurches. "How could you do that? I asked you to keep an eye on it. Everything was in there. My laptop, my tablet."

Joey's face suddenly pales. "Our tickets were in the front pocket of the backpack."

My stomach squeezes even tighter. Our tickets. Our way to Roswell. Gone.

Nadia kneels on the floor and presses her fingers to her forehead. "Okay. It's okay."

"No, it's not okay. We're out the money, our tickets, and all your stuff." Joey throws me another glare, as if the last one has worn off already.

"I'm sorry," I repeat, my voice cracking. "I didn't mean to do it."

"It's okay," Nadia repeats, firmer this time. She looks up at my brother. "It's okay. We'll figure something out. It's not like Jordie did it on purpose."

"He should've kept an eye on them," Joey snaps.

"I know." She stands, brushes off her skirt even though it has no dirt on it. "But there's nothing we can do about it now, so there's no reason to fight about it."

Joey grits his teeth so hard I hear it, then he spins around and stalks off, disappearing out the automatic doors again.

As soon as he's gone, Nadia turns to me. "He's right, you know."

"What? If you agreed with him, why'd you stand up for me?"

"Because arguing about it isn't logical. It's not going to do anything, and we don't really have the time to waste."

I frown. "If you're talking about the bus leaving, I think we're already not getting on that bus now."

"I'm talking about you and Joey having disappeared. Your foster mom will call in and say she hasn't seen you since yesterday morning. Eventually, the school will call and say you guys didn't come in today. After twenty-four hours, the police will get involved. Then you're looking at missing posters and your picture online."

The more she talks, the more I can literally feel the blood stalling in my body. I hadn't even thought of that. If we cause that kind of trouble, there's no way a family will be willing to take in both of us. It'll be another mark against us, another reason for people to say they don't want us.

"Oh crap." I lean forward in my chair, resting my elbows on my thighs so I can put my head in my hands. How could I have let this happen? I get in trouble all the time for not paying attention or for daydreaming in school, but it never really mattered. I wasn't doing anything so important that zoning out would cause a huge problem.

"It's all right." Nadia sits in the chair next to mine and pats me awkwardly on the back. She's not as good at giving comfort as Joey is, but I doubt my brother's going to come rushing in here to do that right now.

"I can't believe I did something so stupid."

"You're not stupid." Another awkward back pat. "You should've been paying attention, but you're not stupid."

"You wouldn't have let the stuff get stolen."

"No, I wouldn't." She says it with so much certainty that my face heats again.

"He's going to make us go back to Payson."

"He's not." She takes her hand off my back and folds it with her other one in her lap. "He knows if you guys go back, you're most likely going to be separated, and he doesn't want to risk it."

I pull my head out of my hands so I can face her. "You still haven't found anything?"

"No, but I will." She nods decisively. "I just need more time. It's a little slower going without my laptop."

I wish I had that much confidence in all of this. I have confidence in the idea of going to Roswell, but not how we're going to get there. And I can't lose Joey.

"You know, it's actually not all that common for siblings to stay together this long in the system. Maybe if you guys lost your parents when you were older, it would be. But Joey says you guys were put in the system before you were even a year old. Lots of places split babies up because they haven't actually formed that sibling bond yet. It's kind of a miracle you guys have managed to stay together this long."

"I know." We've been told for a while now about how lucky we are that we get to stay together. But honestly, I don't feel all that lucky. Because that "luck" is something a lot of people are oblivious to. Most kids don't have to worry about being separated from their brother or sister. So why should I? Why should Joey?

"Is there something you guys aren't telling me?" Nadia asks, leaning forward just slightly so she can look me in the eye. "A reason why they've kept you two together for so long?"

I shake my head. "We're just lucky, Nadia. Camilla's managed to find people who're willing to take in both of us. I guess I thought she always would."

Her hand returns to my back for a slightly less awkward pat. "Well, I'm sure we'll find something in Roswell."

She doesn't say the rest. That if we don't, our options are to keep moving east, or to go back to Payson. We have no money, so we wouldn't get that far east at all. And Payson . . . if they're going to separate me and Joey, that's not really much of an option.

I look around the bus station, at the morning sun starting to stream in through the windows. Is staying in Las Cruces an option? Well . . . it wouldn't be that different from Payson. We'd still have no family and no real home.

The automatic doors slide open, and Joey reappears, his mouth set in a grim line.

"Come on," he says when he reaches us. "We have to start walking if we hope to make it to Roswell."

THIRTEEN

"Walk?" Nadia asks as we head out into the bright New Mexico sun. I already miss the AC in the bus station.

"It's not like we have another choice," Joey says, with a not-so-hidden glare in my direction.

"It's a hundred and eighty-four miles," I point out, remembering it from the route we saw on Nadia's phone.

"Yeah, that's a long walk. If only we had bus tickets."

Nadia puts a hand on my brother's arm. "He didn't mean it, Joey."

He huffs but doesn't say anything else.

I tune him out and try to calculate how long it could take to walk to Roswell, and it's not looking good for us. But I'm not going to point it out to Joey. I'm afraid that if one more bad thing happens, he'll call it quits on this whole thing.

Nadia had told me that Joey wouldn't make us go back to Payson, but there's still a sick feeling in my stomach. Because what if she's wrong? Joey's never shied away from adventure or doing something that isn't too smart, but this is different.

We're a pretty sorry crew straggling down the city streets until we reach the highway. The cars rushing by flip Nadia's hair up all over the place, until she makes us stop so she can pull it up high in a bun at the top of her head.

Half an hour down the road, the first car stops for us.

Nadia waves them on. As much as I want to reach Roswell, I'm thankful she does. I don't like the way the guy in the passenger seat looked at the three of us.

But an hour later, Joey's finished the last of our water, and my skin aches from being under the sun so long. We had to have at least made some serious progress, but when I ask Nadia how far we've gone, she just shakes her head. From the way her lips are pressed so tightly together, I think she's regretting telling Joey to lay off yelling at me.

I open my mouth to apologize again, but then shut it. Saying I'm sorry isn't going to make the situation any better. Besides, my throat's really dry, so I don't think I should try talking again anyway.

Desperation has settled into Joey's eyes. His cheeks are red from the heat, and sweat dots his forehead. So I'm barely surprised when he approaches the red pickup truck that slows on the side of the road.

But it's not desperation that has me following the short stretch of pavement to the side of the truck. It's that while we weren't raised in a typical home, we were still taught stranger danger. And if Joey gets pulled into a car by some serial killer, I'm going with him.

There are two teenagers in the front seat, with a little girl sitting between them. The teenage girl in the passenger seat gives us a bright smile when we reach the window. "Hey, you kids okay?"

"Yeah," Joey says, even though I think it's really obvious

we're not. We're sweaty and covered in road dust from walking so close to passing cars.

The girl's eyebrows draw down like she's thinking the same thing. "Where y'all headed?"

"Roswell," Joey answers. "We had our bus tickets stolen."

He doesn't even cut me a glare when he says it, so I guess he's really tired.

"Well, we're going as far as Ruidoso," the teenage boy driving the pickup says. "We'd be glad to take you guys with us. There's room in the back."

"That'd be great," Joey says. "Thank you."

Next to me, Nadia's eyes are bugging out. She grabs my elbow and reaches for Joey, but he's already lowering the truck tailgate so he can climb into the bed.

"This isn't safe," Nadia hisses out of the side of her mouth. "These people are total strangers."

"We don't have much of a choice," I answer, shaking her hand off. "And they seemed really nice." Our options are too limited to argue about this. Even if it feels like a really bad idea.

I pull myself up into the bed of the truck, then Joey and I reach down to help Nadia. Her skirt doesn't exactly allow for her to hike a leg high enough to climb onto the truck with us. She grunts when we drag her up. Probably because we accidentally hit her shins on the tailgate.

Once we're settled, the truck jerks forward, bumping over the curb, and then we're off. For the first few minutes I sit between Nadia and Joey, expecting the guy to turn off sharply somewhere and lead us to some dark, secluded cabin where he'll hold us for ransom. And we don't even have a family to pay it.

But the time drags on and the sun rises high in the clear blue sky. The heat beats down on my face, but it feels good after spending so many hours on the bus yesterday.

Even Nadia starts to relax, but she still keeps her phone clutched tight in her hand. I wonder if she's starting to regret coming with us on this trip. And how on earth is she supposed to get home if all our money is gone?

I glance to my left, where Joey's face is turned to the sky, his eyes shut against the sun. Maybe he can figure out a way to get more money, to get Nadia home before she gets into trouble. But would she? Every time she talks about her parents, they seem okay.

On my right, Nadia uses her hand to shield the screen on her phone from the sun. She's frowning, her eyebrows drawn together in worry.

"What's wrong?" I ask, having to raise my voice just a little to be heard over the wind whistling by us.

"Nothing." She clicks her phone off. "We really need to get somewhere that I can get a computer. It's easier to research that way. And my battery's way down."

"I'm sorry I lost it," I say, the guilt nipping at my stomach again. Joey and I already don't have a lot, and then I went and lost everything we had. And Nadia's stuff.

"It's okay," Nadia says, tucking a stray strand of hair behind her ear.

Joey gives a low noise, like he's saying she shouldn't let me off the hook so easily. It's not like him. Joey's pretty easygoing—you can tell from how many gross things he's done for dares—and he never holds stuff against me. But I don't blame him for being extra mad at me for this. I deserve it.

The truck hits a pothole and the three of us bounce, hard enough for us to grab at each other's knees, as if that'll keep us in the truck. Nadia's skin is warm beneath my palm. Joey's is sweaty and sticky.

Nadia lets out a little squeak and drops her hand onto mine, squeezing it tightly.

Once the truck rights itself, we look at each other. I take in Joey's flushed face, Nadia's wide eyes. Then Joey snorts and starts laughing, which makes me do the same.

It feels weird to smile after this morning, but my chest lightens. And then Nadia chuckles too, and her shoulders relax. She lets go of my hand, straightens her skirt, and smooths her hair back from her face. "We'll be in Ruidoso in under an hour. We need to regroup and think of our next plan. And I want it to go on record that I think accepting rides from strangers again is a terrible idea."

"We could walk," I suggest. "It's only like an hour's drive there, right?"

"It's seventy-five miles," Nadia answers. "From what I saw on my phone, that could take us like three to four days to get there. And that's being generous."

Oh. Well, at least she had the idea too and actually looked it up. Otherwise, I'd feel like that was a really dumb suggestion.

"We could buy more bus tickets," Joey says.

"With what money?" Nadia asks.

He hesitates for a long minute, watching the flat landscape pass on the other side of the truck. "I could steal it."

"What?" she demands, sitting up straight. "No way. Have you done that before?"

"No, not outright." He picks at a hole starting in the thigh of his shorts. "I'm good at games and stuff though. I could win money."

She frowns, and I can see it on her face, the way she weighs what we need against her own morals. I've seen Joey play games, and no one is *forcing* people to bet money. Just like how he doesn't force other people to dare him. He's just good at that.

"Maybe," she finally relents. "But would we have the time?"

"No, probably not." Joey chews on his lower lip, staring out at the dry plains zipping by on the opposite side of the road.

The truck bounces again, making the key ring in Joey's pocket dig into my thigh. As soon as it does, an idea pops into my head.

I turn to look at Joey, and he's already looking at me, already knows what I'm going to say.

"Vending machines." The words are out of my mouth quickly, nearly carried away on the wind.

"What about them?" Nadia asks.

"When we didn't have money for food, and I couldn't get any through games or dares, I'd open the vending machine."

Nadia's eyes widen. "You'd just steal money?"

"Do I sound like I'm proud of it?" Joey asks.

"Yeah, a little."

The corners of his lips twitch up. "Well, I guess I am. I mean, I can pick one of those in a minute."

"Well . . ." Nadia hesitates. "I guess it's better than nothing. Those machines do often keep money and not give out what you buy."

She shifts, clearly still a little uncomfortable with the plan, but she's committed to getting us to Roswell, to finding a way to keep me and Joey together. And for the few weeks I've known her, I've already realized she doesn't go back on her word.

FOURTEEN

As soon as the couple drops us off in front of a grocery store in Ruidoso, Nadia uses her phone to lead us to a rest stop. It's almost noon, so the sun beats down on all three of us, and I can feel it burning the back of my neck as we make our way down the road.

Once we get there, Joey leaves us under the shade of a fir tree a parking lot over, telling us we'll only mess up his concentration. Then he disappears after giving us an order not to go anywhere. He looks pointedly at me when he says that.

Nadia and I find a patch of grass that's not too directly in the sun and lie back. My legs are a little sore from riding in that pickup, but it beat walking. I throw an arm over my eyes because even with them shut, the sun is still too bright.

"How long do you think it'll take him?" Nadia asks.

"Not long."

"How often does he do it?"

"Not often. We only do it when we really need it. Usually he can get money through dares or bets." I move my arm and turn my head so I can look at her, the need to defend my brother rising up in me. "He's not a thief, you know. He'd never steal it from someone's pocket or something."

"I believe you." She frowns up at the sky. "He's pretty fearless."

I put my arm back over my eyes. "Yeah, that's Joey."

Despite his bravado at getting that ride from strangers in Las Cruces, I could tell he was antsy about it. When we were waiting for Nadia to use the bathroom in that grocery store, Joey looked at me and told me never to take a ride from a stranger unless he was there too. I made him promise the same. It doesn't matter that he's the older one of us, if we're not together, we can't protect each other from the rest of the world.

"So, tell me honestly. Why're you guys going to Roswell? Is that where you were born?"

"I don't know where we were born. They found us in a field in Payson."

"Then what's in Roswell?"

I squeeze my eyes shut tighter under my arm. "You'll think it's dumb."

"Perhaps. But I'm with you on this, so you might as well tell me."

"That's not exactly making me want to tell you anything."

She pokes me in the side suddenly, making me jerk. "Come on, Jordie."

"I guess I think it's where we come from."

"You're traveling all this way, risking getting into trouble because you *guess* it's where you're from?"

"Yes."

She's quiet for a long second, then asks, "What makes you think it's where you're from?"

"You're gonna laugh."

"Maybe."

I keep my arm in place so I don't have to see her expression when I tell her. "I think that maybe Joey and I aren't from earth. Like, maybe we're from the same aliens that landed in Roswell in the fifties."

Minutes pass by in silence, and I feel heat creeping up my cheeks and over the back of my neck. I never said that out loud to anyone but Joey. The other kids at school only found out about it because they saw what I was looking up on the tablet or computer.

Why did I tell her? Just because she's coming with us doesn't mean she's not like the others.

"Why do you think that?" she finally asks, her voice so low it almost gets carried away on the slight New Mexico breeze.

"Because we don't fit in anywhere," I mumble, thankful I don't have to look at her. I can feel her questions, the ones she's not asking. The ones she's too nice to ask.

"Lots of people don't fit in anywhere," Nadia says.

"But we were left in a field, in the middle of a crop circle. And we have . . . marks."

"Like what?"

"Symbols. They're on our backs, and they're exactly the same on both of us. There's no way they're birth marks. They're too freakish for that."

"Can I see them?" Her voice is clinical, all business, but I still blush hotter.

"I don't know."

"Oh, come on." She pokes at my side again. Then again and again until I relent and pull my arm off my eyes so I can sit up.

"Okay, fine." I turn so my back is facing her, then I lift my T-shirt up. It's freakishly hot today, so the fabric sticks to my skin.

She's silent for a second, then asks, "Can I touch them?"

"I guess." I've been prodded before. Henry saw the marks and asked about them. Joey didn't let me tell him what I thought about the aliens. I think he was worried Henry wouldn't want us anymore if I talked about it.

Her fingers touch my back, cool against my warm skin. I feel them rise up and down as she glides over the circles.

"They're cool," she says. "Like little crop circles."

"I know." I've never had anyone refer to them as *cool* before. Henry looked pretty shocked when he saw them, and the few foster parents who got a look at them thought they were weird.

"You've had them forever?"

"I . . . don't really know. No one seems to know. But maybe?"

"They're bumpier than I thought they'd be." She runs her fingers over them again, more confident this time. "Joey's are exactly the same?"

"Yeah." I've seen them enough to know them better than my own.

"So you think your family may be in Roswell."

"Yes." Man, why did my voice have to crack when I answered? Why does this stuff bother me so much sometimes?

Nadia lowers her fingers, so I drop my shirt back down. Then I turn to look at the rest stop building again so I don't have to face her.

"For the record, I don't think what you're doing is stupid,"

Nadia says. "I think if your family hasn't come to you yet, you should go out there and look for them."

"But what if there's a reason they haven't come for us? What if . . . they were never planning on coming for us?" I stare straight ahead at the brick building, trying to ignore the burning in my eyes. Nadia is not the person I ever expected to ask that question to.

"Then they're missing out. Probably."

Her answer makes me laugh even though I'm sure she's being totally serious with the "probably" part. I don't think she knows how to be dishonest when she answers a question, but that also is the reason why she was the perfect person to talk to about this. Joey's lied to me before, when he was trying not to upset me. He thinks I don't know, but I do. We tell each other everything, but Joey's not afraid to massage the truth a little.

"I hope you find what you're looking for in Roswell," Nadia says.

"Thanks."

She balances her phone on her knee. "If this is what we're going to Roswell for, bring me up to speed on all your research."

Calum's Guide to Extraterrestrials

In the summer of 1947, rancher WW Mack Brazel discovered debris on his land. At the direction of base army intelligence officer Major Jesse Marcel, the debris was quickly gathered by the Roswell Army Airfield. The speed with which it was done, along with the continued secrecy surrounding the incident, has long been suspected of being a federal cover-up of extraterrestrial life landing on earth.

The men who recovered the debris attributed it to a weather balloon, but Brazel, the rancher whose land it was found on, stated that it was like nothing he had ever seen before, and certainly not akin to a weather balloon. According to the military, it was actually a string of weather balloons with radar reflectors and sonic equipment. In 1994, the files on it—Project Mogul—were declassified in the hopes of debunking the myth that it was a flying saucer that landed on that ranch in New Mexico.

However, Project Mogul had been conveniently so classified that almost no one knew it even existed. So who's to say what it really was?

No press was allowed to inspect the debris up close. People were turned away at the ranch by military personnel. It's also reported that a four- to five-hundred-foot gouge was seen on the ranch where the debris was found.

According to a book published in 1992, *Crash at Corona*, it's believed that at least two aliens survived the wreck and were taken into government custody. And as for what happened to those poor souls, there's no happy ending.

FIFTEEN

We only stop reading when the battery light on Nadia's phone starts flashing, signaling she only has about five percent left.

She turns the screen off, then places her phone facedown on the grass beside her. "Wow."

"I know."

"Everyone's heard of the UFO sightings in Roswell, but I didn't realize there was so much to it. And there's even more I have to read through." Her hand twitches toward her phone, but she pulls it back to her lap quickly. "We have to get a charger so I can keep going."

"So you believe it's possible?"

She lifts her glasses so she can rub her left eye with her index finger. "I think a lot of things are possible. That's not the right question. What we need to know is if it's *plausible*."

"What's the difference?"

"'Possible' means it might've happened, but we need to know if it's feasible. If it *could* have happened, instead of maybe it did." She lowers her glasses back to the bridge of her nose and stares out at the empty parking lot. "It's pretty crazy, Jordie."

My shoulders drop even though I was expecting her to say that. "I know."

"That doesn't mean it's not plausible." She gives me a smile, then pats the pockets on her suit jacket. When she pulls out a pen and paper, my spirits lift a little. I've seen her do this before, take notes about something other than schoolwork. It means she thinks there really is something to learn, something to think through.

"First, can aliens actually reproduce?"

My ears turn hot. "Nadia."

"It's a logical question. Second, if aliens are gray or green with massive eyes and weird limbs and fingers, why do you and Joey look like humans?"

"A lot of people think that all the alien abductions and testing were done so aliens could learn how to look like people. It's not really too far of a reach to think that they could create a very human-looking alien."

She scratches beneath her bun with the end of the pen. "That's a good point. And logical. I mean, if they have superior technology to ours, there's probably not a lot they can't do. Okay, so third, what do the circles on your back mean? Have you ever found anyone with an alien abduction encounter who mentioned aliens having markings close to that?"

"No," I admit. "But maybe they're not visible on them?"

"Hmm." She chews on the end of the pen before circling the question. "We'll have to come back to that. Fourth, if you are from outer space, why were you left in a field?"

"Maybe it was an accident."

She glances at me, and I watch her eyes soften a little. "I think if it were an accident, they would've come back for you by now."

I look away from her. I'd already thought of that. "I know."

"It's okay," she says bracingly. "If it wasn't an accident, there had to be a reason. Maybe it's another kind of test? If they've been doing physical tests on people for years, maybe this is another kind, to see how well they can get you guys to blend in."

I think of the way Joey eats bugs on dares, and how we can't seem to find anyone who wants us. "I don't know if we're doing too great of a job at that. Maybe that's why they haven't come back for us yet."

Another circle. "We'll think on that one too. Fifth, what else besides the marks makes you think you might be a product of aliens?"

"I don't know." I draw a line through the dirt with my index finger, avoiding a beetle that's crawling through the soil. "It's a feeling, I guess. We're just . . . different."

"I'm not denying that." She scribbles on her paper. "But, come on, you have to have something."

"I can't remember the first seven years of my life," I say. "Joey can only remember bits and pieces."

She frowns. "Okay, that is unusual."

"When we were on the bus to Las Cruces, I had a memory of my mom."

She looks up, her eyes wide behind her glasses. "And? What happened?"

I think back to the cool hand holding mine, to the lights and the glare at that burn. "I think I was on a ship. The lights were spinning and she was talking about how I needed to go."

"Is that your only memory?"

"Yeah."

"Does Joey have any?"

"He hasn't told me, but I think he would if he did." I try to make myself sound more confident than I actually feel. The truth is, I don't know if Joey would tell me. It might be another time he massaged the truth so he didn't have to admit something. But Joey wants a family too, I know he does. If he had a memory or something that would help, he would tell me.

"What did she look like?"

"I don't know. I couldn't really tell. I think I was really young."

"Is it uncommon for the state not to have located either one of your birth parents by now?"

I frown. "I don't know. I never thought much about that, about if it was weird for them to not find either one. I guess I thought if they wanted to be found, they would be."

The end of the pen goes back into her mouth and she chomps on it. "Have they ever taken blood samples or anything for DNA testing?"

"Yeah, sure. Maybe four years ago or so." After I got a look at the needle, I got so light-headed I thought I might pass out. Joey had to stand beside me and keep telling me it would be okay.

"And nothing?"

"Nothing so far, I guess. I think they would've told us if they'd found something." I hope they would tell us. "If they found something, we wouldn't be the state's problem anymore."

Nadia stares at me, her brow furrowed. "Is that really how they teach you to talk about yourselves? As problems?"

Her question surprises me. "No. Camilla's pretty cool. I just . . . I don't know. Getting passed from home to home, not finding someone who'll keep you that long, it makes you feel like a problem, even if no one calls you it."

I shut my mouth. I didn't mean to tell her all of that. She should've told me she was that easy to talk to. Because it doesn't come across when you first meet her.

"That's a really terrible way to live," she says bluntly.

I shrug. I don't want to complain because I know it could be worse. And I have Joey. We met other foster kids without siblings. I don't know what I would do without him.

"We'll figure it out," she says, then raises a hand and points to the rest stop building. "Look, Joey's coming. He looks happy."

Yeah. He's doing his money walk. There's a bounce in his step and a grin has pulled his mouth wide.

As soon as he reaches us, his smile broadens even further. "I got the money for bus tickets. And some food. I don't know about you guys, but I'm starving."

"Did you get enough to buy a charger for my phone?" Nadia asks when we stand.

"Maybe. Depends on how much food you eat."

She rolls her eyes as we turn away from the rest area. "So how much did you get?"

"Enough," he answers. "And just what we needed, okay? It's not like I took enough to buy a mansion."

"You're awfully defensive about it."

He huffs, but then his smile comes back. I think he likes the way Nadia talks. "Whatever. I think I'll keep track of it all."

My cheeks burn. "I said I was sorry."

He bumps my shoulder with his. "It's okay. I'm mostly over it."

Sixteen

We go to a burger place for lunch. Joey pays in one-dollar bills. His eyes are bright and he looks happier than he has since we left Payson. Probably since even before we left.

Nadia's watching him, her phone next to her on the table, charging with the new cord and adapter we stopped at a gas station to buy. I still feel really bad about losing her stuff. Nadia's not like us; she can buy new stuff if it gets lost or broken. But I know the value of things because Joey and I don't have a lot. I should've been more careful.

"Jordie and I talked about Roswell while you were cleaning out the vending machines."

Joey crams three fries into his mouth. "What about Roswell?"

"About how you guys might've come from there. And he showed me the marks."

Joey pauses with another handful of fries halfway to his mouth. "You showed her?"

"Yeah. She was asking about Roswell."

The fries make it to the end of their journey into Joey's mouth, and he turns his head to stare out the window, still chewing. "So, what do you think about it, Nadia?"

She shrugs. "I think it has enough merit to check it out.

But . . . it doesn't really matter what I think. This is about you and Jordie."

"What about the other thing?" I ask, eager to get off the subject of Nadia looking at the marks on my back. "Have you found anything that might help us stay together if we go back to Payson?"

"Nothing concrete," she admits. "But I'm looking into petitioning. If I'm right, you guys could petition to stay together, even if it means changing cities or even states. But I don't know what all of it entails yet."

A petition. I hadn't thought of that before. Though wouldn't Camilla have mentioned it if it was an option? She's always said she's trying to keep me and Joey together.

"Jordie also told me that you guys had samples taken a while back so they could try and find your biological parents."

"Wow. Can't leave you two alone for three seconds before you spill everything, huh?" Joey smirks when he says it, but the tension in his shoulders makes me think he's a little mad at me for telling that to Nadia.

She puts her elbows on the table and leans forward. "Is it true they never found anything?"

"Yes. What, you think I'd lie to my own brother about that?" He shakes his head. "Camilla told me that happens sometimes."

"There could be a reason for that," I point out.

"Yeah, like maybe the parents live off the grid or something. And besides, lots of people aren't in databases." Joey picks angrily at his fries. "We're already on our way there; you can stop trying to convince me."

Hurt stings my chest. "Why're you being like this?"

Nadia looks between the two of us, then slowly stands. "Um, I'm going to . . . use the bathroom again."

As soon as she disappears, I move out of the seat next to Joey and take Nadia's place so I can face him. "What's going on with you?"

"Nothing." He shrugs.

"Are you mad at me for talking to Nadia about it?"

He pushes his plate away and looks at me. "Why'd you show her? It's not like it's something to be proud of."

My stomach turns. I hadn't realized he looked at it like that. I'm not exactly running around showing it to people, but I don't care if they see it. "It's not something to be . . . not proud of."

Joey shakes his head, his lips curling with something that looks like bitterness. It makes him look older. "People don't want to adopt weirdos, okay?"

"Well the last time I checked, Nadia wasn't exactly looking to adopt either one of us." The knot in my stomach tightens, turning even heavier. "Wait, do you think I'm the reason no one wants to keep us?"

"No." His face softens, becoming my brother again. "No, Jordie, of course that's not what I think. It's just . . . you saw Marian's face when she got a look at those marks. Like we were devils or something."

I picture that foster mom's face in my head, her eyes wide and her lips curled in disgust. "Yeah, I remember that."

He picks at the wrapper his burger came in. "I just want you to be careful, that's all."

"I know. But Nadia's not like that. She didn't make a big deal out of them."

He nods, but I can't help feeling like he's still not happy. His earlier joy at getting money back is gone, replaced with the frown I usually only see on him when we're being shuttled to a new home.

"I'm sorry," I say when the silence feels like too much. I wish Nadia would stop hiding out in the bathroom.

"It's okay." He doesn't take his fries back, so I don't think it's okay. Still, when Nadia gets back to the table (finally), he gives her the same smile he uses on Camilla when she's asking if we'll be on our best behavior with a new family.

I think he's lying without words.

Calum's Guide to Extraterrestrials

There's some evidence that crop circles were first seen as early as the 1600s. However, the term "crop circle" wasn't coined until the '80s, when several hundred crop circles were being discovered every year.

Some have since been attributed to Dave and Doug, two kids who started making crop circles with tools in 1978. But while they came forward in the '90s, it can only explain a handful of the circles. They didn't make circles all over the world, and no one else came forward.

Even those who scoff at crop circles being linked to alien landings can't deny that there's a marked military interest in crop circles. They don't hesitate to fly helicopters over the sites, and take samples.

In the early '90s, a biophysicist ran tests on some of the stalks taken from the crop circles. The crops weren't broken, but bent. The biophysicist discovered that the apical nodes on the plants had lengthened a considerable amount, which can be attributed to electromagnetic exposure. This exposure sometimes affected only one row of the nodes, which is something that can't be duplicated by anything on earth.

SEVENTEEN

J oey sleeps on the bus ride to Roswell. My stomach is too
full of nerves to even think about sleeping. I'm also thankful
he's in the seat between me and Nadia again. I feel weird after
having shown her the marks on my spine. While it didn't seem
to bother her, Joey's reaction bothered me. I don't think he's
ever been so upset with me before as he has been on this trip.

I need to stop screwing up.

On Joey's other side, Nadia's phone starts ringing, blaring
out some orchestra music.

She frowns at the screen. "It's my dad. He's not supposed
to call until tonight."

The music wakes Joey, and he sits upright, looking around
quickly. I watch the recognition fill his eyes as he remembers
where we are, and he runs a hand down his face, trying to
wipe away the sleep.

Unfortunately, that's how both of us usually wake up.
We've been moved around so much that sometimes, it feels
like we never stop. Maybe that's why Joey's so comfortable
sleeping on buses.

Nadia answers the call and presses the phone to her ear.
"Hey, Dad."

I watch her face while her dad says something to her. It's

too low for me to hear the words, but Nadia's eyebrows scrunch together.

"Two boys from school?" she asks. "No, Dad, I've been home."

My body tenses. Next to me, Joey's does the same. They're already looking for us. I'd counted on Katie not saying anything about it for a couple days. It's not like she's ever cared that much.

For all Nadia's smarts, she's a pretty bad liar. Her voice is too high, and she's fidgeting like crazy, touching her nose, playing with her glasses. "No, Dad, I'm fine," she says. "I just may be getting sick. Don in my English class was sick yesterday. They sent him to the nurse's office."

Her voice evens out when she says that, so it's probably true.

"I will," she says into the phone. "Okay. I'll talk to you later. Bye."

As soon as she ends the call, she sucks in a shaky breath. "He's going to find out soon that I lied. He'll call the nanny I'm supposed to be with."

"Are you going to get in trouble?" I ask. Joey and I have a lot of experience with that.

"No. He'll be more upset and worried than angry."

Oh. Joey and I don't exactly have a lot of experience with that.

"Can you tell him you're staying with a friend?" Joey asks.

"Yeah, but it won't matter. He'll call and check with her mom, and then I'll have lied to him again." She runs a hand across her forehead, pressing on the skin. "I don't like lying to my parents."

"Then when we get to Roswell, we'll buy you a ticket to go back home," I say.

"No." Her mouth drops like she can't believe I would suggest that. "I'm not leaving, not when we're almost here, and certainly not when we get there. We're going to Roswell for answers, and I promised to help you find them."

"But we don't want you to get in trouble," Joey replies. "We'd rather you go home."

"No." She crosses her arms over her chest, as if that'll make the conversation stop.

"Nadia—"

"It'll be fine," she interrupts me. "When Dad calls back, I won't answer. Not until we get to Roswell. Then I'll tell him. He'll want me to come back, but I'll get a ticket for a bus that's not leaving until tomorrow night. That way we have the whole day to look. It's not as much as I wanted, but it'll have to do."

"Then what?" Joey asks.

"What do you mean?" I turn to look at him. "We'll have answers by tomorrow night, and Nadia will be on her way home. What else is there to talk about?"

Joey glances between the two of us, and I catch the grimace on his face before he can hide it. "What if we don't find the answers by tomorrow night?"

"Then we'll keep looking," I say. Heat is starting to rise in my neck, on its way to my cheeks. Why does he keep pushing this? "It's not like we can go back to Payson anyway."

"Do you understand what's going to happen to us if you're wrong about Roswell?" Joey's voice is low, quieter than I think I've ever heard it. "We pretty much blew our chance in Payson. We'll be homeless."

"It's not like people were lining up to take us in," I snap. "And you think it's 'cause I let too many people know about the alien stuff, right?"

"Are you really bringing that up?" Joey asks. "I said it's not what I meant."

"Then what did you mean?" Angry tears prick my eyes, but I blink them away. There's no way I'm crying in front of either one of them right now, especially Joey.

Nadia's looking around the bus frantically, probably wishing she had another bathroom to go hide in.

"I just meant that it wouldn't be so bad if we behaved normally, instead of you always insisting that our parents are from freaking outer space."

I jerk back, but it's not because he's yelling. It's because he's never said something like that to me. I knew the alien stuff bothered him a little, but I didn't realize it was that bad.

Before I have the chance to respond, the bus jerks to a stop at the station. Nadia grabs our one bag and stands quickly. "Come on, boys, come on. Got a lot of ground to cover."

We follow her out, and I shield my eyes against the sun.

Joey won't look at me. His cheeks have red splotches on them, like they always do when he's angry.

I check the time on Nadia's phone when she flips the screen up. About forty minutes until I'm supposed to meet Calum for lunch. There's no way I can take Joey with me. I can't do anything else with him until I have real proof.

"I have to go to the bathroom," I say when we step into the air-conditioned bus station.

"Okay." Nadia gives a bright, false smile. "I'll wait here."

Joey doesn't say anything. He won't be coming with me like he did at the last bus station. But that's okay.

I have twenty bucks Joey slipped in my pocket back in Las Cruces, and I know the diner I'm supposed to go to isn't that far from here.

I take a breath and push my shaking hands into my pockets. Then I head for the back exit of the bus station without looking back.

EIGHTEEN

It's super hot out, so by the time I reach the diner, with six minutes to spare, my shirt is sticking to me. I grab the door and step into the café, pulling in a deep breath of the ice-cold air conditioner.

There are rows of booths and tables on one wall, and the other one has a really long red bench with small square tables in front of it. In the other direction is a bar with stools. There's a cool old Coke machine behind the back booths.

I recognize Calum immediately from his blog. His dark skin is glistening thanks to sunlight slanting in through the window he's next to. Two older guys sit opposite him in the booth.

The little bit of spit I have left in my mouth dries up, and sweat breaks out on my palms. But I tuck my fear back in and approach their table.

"Hi." It comes out as a whisper, but Calum still looks up. He gives me a hesitant smile when he says, "Hi."

"I'm, um, the guy from the blog."

"Oh." His smile widens, and he holds out a hand for me to shake. It feels weird because I've only ever known old guys to do that, and Calum looks like he's in college. Still, I shake his hand.

"Grab a chair," he says. "Join us."

I do what he says, sitting on the edge of it. I feel weird being here without Joey. We've been lots of places apart, but we always knew where the other one was. For the first time, I feel guilty for leaving Joey at the bus station without telling him where I was going. If he'd done that to me, I'd be freaked out.

"Um, one second," I say, then stand.

Calum nods, and then I make my way to the bar at the back, where a woman in a uniform of a white button-down and pink skirt is typing something up.

"Hi, do you have a phone I could borrow? I . . . lost mine." It's always easier to say that than to tell people that you don't have one. It always makes them look at you weird, like it's abnormal for kids to not have phones.

The lady gives me a smile and lifts an old phone onto the bar, the kind that you have to stick your finger in a hole and spin to dial. "There you go, honey."

"Thank you." I pull it toward me and dial Nadia's cell phone number. She made me and Joey memorize it on the bus ride from Phoenix to Las Cruces in case we got separated.

She answers on the first ring. "Hello?"

"Nadia? It's Jordie."

"Jordie? Where the heck are you? Joey and I are going crazy. He was scared someone took you."

My stomach twists again with fresh guilt. "I'm sorry. I just didn't want to fight with him anymore."

"Okay." I hear her take a deep breath and let it out slowly. "Okay. Where are you? We'll meet up with you."

I give her directions to the store across the street. I don't want either one of them seeing Calum. Not until I know if he can help me or not.

"Just stay there," she says. "We'll be there as soon as we can."

I hang up the phone, thank the lady behind the counter again, then make my way back to Calum's table.

"Everything okay?" he asks when I sit down.

"Yeah, I just had to call a friend."

He studies me for a long second, then says, "I have to say, I expected you to be older. You don't talk like a . . . how old are you?"

"Twelve," I answer.

"Yeah, you don't talk like a twelve-year-old." He turns to the guys in the booth across from him. "These are my friends, Lewis and Tony. They're in college with me."

I give them a smile that they both return, Lewis more shyly than Tony.

"So." Calum picks up a sugar packet and hits it against his palm a couple times before ripping it open and dumping the contents into his black coffee. "What can we help you with?"

"Do you really believe in all this stuff? The aliens and the UFOs and them walking among us?"

"Yes, of course. I wouldn't be running a blog about it if I didn't." He takes a sip of his coffee, frowns, then reaches for another sugar packet. "But that's not what you wanted to ask me. Don't be shy. You came all the way out here for a reason."

"I need to find proof," I say. "It's really important that someone I know believes that aliens exist, and that they run tests. That they can look like humans."

"It's hard to convince a nonbeliever," Calum warns.

"I know, but I have to." I sigh, remembering my fight with

Joey on the bus earlier. "You said on your blog that you lived with someone who'd been abducted. You talked about how people who have experiences with aliens are treated."

"Yeah." He clears his throat, and both his friends drop their gazes to the table. Lewis picks up a straw wrapper and winds it around his pointer finger.

Calum is quiet for so long that fear starts eating at my stomach. "Sorry," I finally say when the silence keeps growing. "I shouldn't have brought it up."

"No, no, it's okay. I invited you here so we could talk about aliens." He rolls his shoulders like he's preparing for a fight or something. "My dad was the one who was abducted. I was eight when it happened. He went out of the house to grab something from his car, and he never came back inside. When my mom went out to check on him, the car door was open and the lights were on. We didn't see him until the next day, when a jogger found him on the side of the road outside a forest. He was dehydrated, but otherwise okay."

My mouth is dry. I want to tell him to stop talking. Because all I can picture is Joey getting grabbed like that in the middle of the night. What would I do if something like that happened?

"I think you're scaring him," Lewis says softly.

I shake my head to pull myself together. "No, I'm fine." I look back at Calum. "What happened after he was found?"

"Well, I'm sure you've already guessed that no one believed him when he talked about the spaceship or the aliens."

"What did he say about the aliens?"

"Not much. His memory was a little spotty about them.

He did say they didn't hurt him, that they just ran some tests, took some blood. He said it wasn't scary."

"So you think maybe they're not bad?"

Calum shrugs. "They're like humans, some good, some bad."

That makes me feel better about being related to aliens. They're shown in movies a lot as scary, but I think our mom and dad must be more like the alien from the movie *E.T.*

"Listen, if you need help convincing someone, then you should take him to talk to Red on the Coleman Ranch. Red saw a landing last year in his pasture. There's also Beth out by the quarry. And Alvin, who lives by the lake. All three of them have firsthand accounts of it. Alvin was there when the one in 1947 landed. He was working as a ranch hand at the place where it crashed."

Wow. So he has to be like a bazillion years old by now.

"Did any of them see other humans on the ship?"

"Not that they mentioned."

"Which one do you think would be the most helpful? I'm not sure I can make it to talk to all three of them."

Calum frowns, his gaze flicking toward the ceiling as he thinks. "Alvin or Beth probably. Alvin's been around the longest and his memory's the sharpest, but Beth's only happened a few years ago. And I think she remembers the most about the ship."

I hesitate, playing with the empty sugar packets. "Do you know about any UFO sightings or stuff in Arizona? Around the Phoenix area?"

"Sure, there were a few. There are also crop circles out

JUDI LAUREN

there that aren't made by humans. It's possible there've actually been more than a few landings out there."

"Did you see the one from Payson?" I don't feel embarrassed asking him the question, not when he believes in their existence so fully.

"Oh yeah. That was a big one. That was where they found those twin babies." He shakes his head. "I wonder what happened to them. I'd kill to talk to them."

I don't tell him I'm one of them. I don't want to risk it, not when I don't know Calum that well.

"I have pictures of it," Calum says, pulling out his cell phone. "My dad actually traveled there and took these. He's kind of the reason I'm into all this stuff."

I try to imagine having a dad who's so into something that it passes down to me or Joey. My gaze shifts out the window to the store across the street, even though I know there's no way Nadia and Joey have made it there yet.

"Here it is." Calum puts his phone on the table and spins it to face me. "They called it the 'bull's-eye circles.' Two of them side by side."

I stare at the aerial photo. It looks like it was taken from a helicopter. "When did he take this?"

"The day after the farmer found the circle."

The rings look like the marks on my spine, only a lot bigger. They're not an exact match, but they're close enough to make the hair on the back of my neck stand up. "Can I show you something?"

"Sure." Calum pockets his phone again and looks up as I

102

stand. When I start pulling my shirt up, his eyes widen. "Hey, kid—"

I turn before he can get any more out and show him my back. It silences him almost immediately. Fortunately, we're in a back booth, so no one's paying any attention to us.

"Whoa." Lewis leans over the table to get a better look at my back. "Where did you get those?"

"I've had them for as long as I can remember." My voice sounds small, but I don't try to change it. First Nadia, now these guys. Joey would crap if he saw me doing this. Maybe it would show him how desperate I really am.

"Can I touch them?" Calum asks.

"Yeah."

His fingers are just as warm as Nadia's, but they feel different. A little bolder as they run over my raised skin.

"I've never seen anything like this," he says. "These are amazing."

If he lived with them, I don't think he'd believe they were so amazing. "You've never seen anything similar?"

"Maybe. Hang on, I'll check. Hey, can I take a photo of these?"

"Um . . . I-I don't know."

"I wouldn't put it on the blog. It's just for me to study."

The idea of him having a photo of these makes my stomach twist. "I guess. But only if it's a close-up of just the mark."

I stand still while he takes the photo, then I drop my shirt and sit in the chair again. Lewis and Tony are looking at each other like they're trying to read one another's mind. My stomach turns again, so I cross my arms over it. "I know they're pretty freaky looking."

"Are you kidding?" Lewis asks with a smile. "Those were cool. Seriously."

My cheeks warm, so I check out the window again. Still no sign of Nadia or my brother.

"They look similar to the rings in Payson," Calum says, flipping back and forth between the two photos. He shows the one he took of mine, where the only thing actually visible is the mark. I can't even see any surrounding unmarked skin. "Though on you, there's a missing chunk out of all the outer circles, and there's not in the field ones."

"What about on other people?"

"Actually, Beth has a mark," Calum says. "She has two on her shoulders. They don't look like this, but they're circles. She didn't have them before the abduction."

"What do you think they're from?"

"She mentioned some testing. You should really talk to her though. It's completely different when you're talking to someone who actually lived it." He clicks his phone off and studies my face. "You're sure you don't know where those marks came from?"

I nod.

"Where are you from?" When I don't answer, he says, "I'm guessing somewhere in north Arizona."

"I'm missing large pieces of my memory," I say softly, my throat tight for some stupid reason. "I just want to know where it went."

"Then you should talk to Beth and Alvin." His voice gentles. "Don't worry. They're not known to take the same people twice. They won't come back for you."

How am I supposed to tell him that them not coming back for me is exactly what I'm afraid of?

Nineteen

I wait at the store for seven minutes before Joey and Nadia show up. Their faces are red and sweaty. Joey's hair is sticking to his forehead. As soon as he reaches me, he punches me hard in the shoulder. "Don't do that again," he snaps. Then he hugs me.

Behind him, Nadia tucks her own flyaway hair behind her ears and clears her throat. "I'm glad you're all right, Jordie. Please don't leave again without telling us where you're going."

"I won't," I promise.

Joey steps back from me. "Nadia, I need to talk to Jordie alone for a sec."

She holds her hand out palm up. "Give me a few bucks. I'll get us some snacks."

He pulls the bills out from the front pocket of his shorts and hands them to her. As soon as she's gone, he grips my elbow and steers me to a metal bench near the door. "Why did you leave without telling us? Were you really that mad at me?"

"I didn't do it to upset you," I say. "I just needed some time to think."

"You could've done that just a few feet away from me." Hurt is in his words, even though he tries to hide it.

"I'm sorry." The guilt comes back, weighted and hot. "I shouldn't have made you worry."

"No, you shouldn't have." He stretches his legs out. "And you left me with Nadia telling me I should've been nicer to you."

"I hope you listened to her." I elbow his side.

He laughs. "I shouldn't have lost it on you. I'm sorry."

"It's okay."

"So where've you been? You didn't hang out here the whole time."

I hesitate, my mind flashing back to the last conversation we had, when he partially blamed our situation on me talking about aliens. But he said he was sorry.

"I was talking to someone."

"And?" Joey prompts when I don't say any more.

I look down at my hands. "And they told me about two people we could maybe talk to. Both saw aliens up close."

My voice comes out smaller than I mean for it to. But I don't want him to yell at me again.

"Okay," Joey says. "Then we'll go talk to them."

"That's it?"

"Yeah. We're losing Nadia soon when she has to get on a bus back to Arizona. We have to use her while we still have her, and fighting isn't going to help us find answers any sooner. I promise I won't fight you anymore on it."

"Thanks, Joey."

He slaps his thighs and straightens on the bench. "Okay. So who're we meeting with first?"

I tell him what Calum told me about Beth and Alvin. How Alvin was there in 1947 when the first ship landed, and about how Beth was taken aboard one of the ships. I try to hear it the way a stranger would, without all the belief that it's real. It does sound pretty out there.

Joey listens and nods. "You want to talk to Alvin first?"

"Okay." It feels weird that he's agreeing to this so quickly. Nadia must've really yelled at him.

When Nadia comes back with sodas and chips and candy, we tell her where we're going.

She falls into step beside us without argument. We head back out into the heat, and mow through a bag of Ruffles in the first five minutes. As we walk, I fill her in on what Calum told me. I leave out that he took a photo of one of the marks. I think it would freak Joey out.

"Okay, so I have an out-there idea," Nadia says. "I think after we talk to Alvin and Beth, we go to Area 51, in Nevada."

"You realize it's guarded by armed men, right?" Joey asks. "They have actual guns. It's a military base."

"I know." She's taken off her suit jacket and has it tied around her waist. Her dress shirt underneath is sleeveless, so her shoulders are turning pink from the sun. "It's not my first choice, obviously. We could get arrested. But I've been doing a lot of thinking about it, and if there are aliens in Area 51, who's to say they're just the ones from Roswell? Isn't it possible that Area 51 is a base where they conduct tests or experiments from aliens found all over the US? And maybe if they're in captivity, it's the reason why they haven't come back for you guys."

Captivity. I'd never thought of that.

"If that's true, then we should go now," I say.

"No, that's a terrible idea," Joey cuts me off before I can get any further. "It's broad daylight. They won't let us in, so we'd have to sneak in. And we can't do that until it's dark out. At least another six hours."

My shoulders drop. He's right. As usual.

"But . . . we will go," Joey says. "We just have to be smart about it. We'll talk to Alvin and Beth first, and then make a plan about getting to Area 51."

So we make our way to the lake, eating the snacks Nadia bought. Her dad calls when the lake comes into view, and she silences her phone. When I look at her, she says, "I'll call him back when we're done talking to Alvin."

If he talks to us. I'm sure lots of people have wanted to talk to him about what he saw in Roswell that day. But he talked to Calum, so maybe he'll be willing to talk to us. I think if I'd seen a UFO up close, I'd want to talk about it.

When we reach his house, I climb the three rickety porch steps and knock loudly on the cabin door.

He answers almost immediately, a pitchfork gripped tight in his hand. "What do you want?"

"To talk to you." It comes out high and squeaky. I clear my throat. "Calum said you might be willing to talk."

He grunts, but lowers the pitchfork. "You here about the Roswell crash?"

We give simultaneous nods.

"You kids shouldn't be digging into that," Alvin says. His white hair stands up straight, like he stuck his finger in an electrical outlet. His hands are leathery where they're wrapped around the pitchfork. "You should let it go."

He starts to close the door, but I move closer, positioning my foot so he can't close it all the way.

"Please," I say. "We just want to talk. We've been traveling for a full day, and we just want your take on what happened that day. It's really important to us."

When he hesitates, I add another "Please."

He relents and widens the door, allowing us to enter. Joey steps in front of me to go first, like he's worried about what'll be on the other side of the door. But there's nothing to worry about.

The cabin is cleaner than I expected it to be. Daylight slants in through the open windows, and it fills the air inside with the scent of the lake. The floors are clean, and there's a thick rug stretched out near the tiny table. It looks like it might be the carcass of a bear, which really freaks me out, so I look away from it.

"Okay," he says once the door is shut behind us. "Let's hear your questions and I'll decide whether or not to answer them."

That doesn't exactly sound promising, but it's the best we're going to get. I shift through the questions in my head. Joey and Nadia stand silently beside me.

"The debris you saw, what did it look like?"

He grunts again, sets the pitchfork by the door. "Silver. It was humming too. They attributed that to the electromagnetic stuff it had on it."

"The kind of stuff they haven't been able to replicate?" I ask.

He nods, surprise filling his eyes that I know that. "Yeah. I've never felt anything like it. It was almost metal, but stronger metal than I'd ever seen. It was cold too, like it had been in ice, even though it was July."

My stomach dips. There's so much sincerity in Alvin's voice. "Were there marks on it?"

He frowns. "Sure, there were some engravings. The government said it was theirs, in a foreign language, but I've studied since then. Nothing like it."

"What did it look like? The engravings?"

He shuffles to a small wooden desk in the corner and opens a drawer. Paper rustles, and then he comes back to me, holding out a handful of copy paper.

Nadia and Joey crowd near me on either side, looking over my shoulders at the drawings. They're hastily done, the lines bold in some areas and faded in others. They're small squares with dots in the middle of them, almost like giant dice.

The next sheet of paper has a tree on it, but the branches are all woven together.

"These were all on the debris?" Joey asks as we flip through a couple more drawings.

"Yep. I had photos, but the government seized those too." He doesn't sound angry or bitter about it. He even shrugs when he says it.

"What happened afterward?" Nadia asks. "After the government was called in and they took the stuff away?"

"Nothing. We had some weird weather; big storms blew in. We had power outages. Our animals didn't like to be left alone. But nothing that was big enough to really look into."

"Do you think it was a UFO?" Some of the skepticism

that's been in Joey's voice when he talked about Roswell has disappeared.

"Yeah." Alvin nods decisively. "I was just a teenager when it happened. As soon as I could, I went off to college. From there, I got a job in military intelligence, and I can tell you right now that we had nothing like that. And despite the rumors, the Russians didn't either."

I hand the papers back to him and he returns to the desk to stuff them in the drawer.

"It was a pretty crazy time," Alvin says, turning back to us. "I spent a lot of my life trying to find out what it really was. I'm not sure we'll ever know."

I nod. "Can I ask you one more question?"

"Shoot." He tucks his hands in the pockets of his overalls.

"Do you think it's possible that there are aliens on earth?"

He's quiet for so long that I think he might not answer. But then he turns his face to look out the window at the lake. "Yeah, kid, I reckon there are."

TWENTY

A lvin had an effect on Joey. I can tell in the way his eyebrows are drawn down, like he's considering all of it.

"What'd you think?" I ask Nadia. She was the quietest one of us in Alvin's cabin.

"He was telling the truth," she answers. "And I think he's still a little scared. It's why he told us not to be digging into it."

"But what's he afraid of?" I ask, shielding my eyes from the afternoon sun so I can turn and take another look at the cabin. Alvin's watching us from the doorframe.

"My guess is it's the unknown. And he dedicated years of his life to finding more like what was discovered in 1947, and he couldn't find anything."

"Plus, they're technically invaders," Joey adds from my other side.

"Yeah, but if they've been around this long and haven't done anything to hurt earth as a whole, doesn't that show that they're not interested in it?"

Nadia frowns, and Joey shrugs.

I try to push the haunted look on Alvin's face from my mind. He said himself that the aliens didn't hurt anyone, and that it was just debris from a ship they found.

"Hang on." I stop and turn back toward the cabin. Alvin's

still watching us. "I'm going to go ask him something else. I'll be right back."

I expect Nadia to argue, or just follow me, but she doesn't. Joey stays beside her, but he does move forward a few steps, like he doesn't want to let me out of his sight.

I jog back to the cabin and climb the steps. "I forgot a question."

"Seems more like it just came to you."

My face heats, but I don't look away from him. "What do you think the aliens want from earth?"

His gaze shifts to the lake on the side of the cabin. The sun is glinting off it, making the surface look like diamonds. "Everyone's got a different opinion on that, kid."

"I know. But I want to hear yours."

He clicks his tongue against his teeth, then jams his hands back into the pockets of his overalls. "They were way more advanced in 1947 than we were. It stands to reason they're still way more advanced than we are today, even with all the stuff we've accomplished. I don't think they're looking to take over. I think they're just . . . looking."

"For what though?"

He shrugs. "What're any of us looking for?"

"If you don't think they're trying to hurt earth, then why would you tell us not to go digging into it?"

"Because you can waste your whole life looking for something like that." He gives me another look. "And because if they are just looking, then that means they're lost. And lost creatures are dangerous and desperate creatures."

TWENTY-ONE

I turn Alvin's words over in my mind the entire walk back to town. Joey and I have been lost practically our whole lives. Does that make us dangerous or desperate? And if it does, is that so bad? I'm tired of not having a family, of changing homes and schools and parents.

I want to belong somewhere, even if that place isn't earth.

We go to an alien-themed restaurant for a late lunch. My stomach is growling, and those chips feel like I ate them twelve hours ago. Plus, my skin is freakishly hot from the long day in the sun.

When we step into the restaurant, I suck down a lungful of the cool air.

We grab a table in the back, and Joey does a quick count of the money we have left, making sure there's enough for bus tickets.

Nadia looks at the bills, her nose wrinkling. "I can't believe I have to go back home."

"You talked to your dad?"

"Not yet. I have to call him back. He left a message for me while we were with Alvin. Let's just say I haven't ever heard him use that tone except when he was talking with clients."

"I'm sorry," I say. A memory of a foster home flashes through my mind. The foster dad was screaming in my face.

I don't even remember what I did. Then there was Carl's dad, who yelled at him and Joey for half an hour when he caught them kissing that day.

My stomach twists with fear. I don't want that for Nadia.

She waves a hand. "It's no big deal. He'll probably ground me. I'm usually very well-behaved."

"You make yourself sound like a pet, you know," Joey says, folding his menu back up.

"You just say that because you don't know how to behave." She heaves a sigh and stands from the table. "I'm going to call Dad. Order me one of those burgers with fries. And I want a Coke."

I nod, and then she disappears into the back of the restaurant.

"So what'd you go back to ask Alvin?" Joey asks.

I watch the waiters and waitresses rush back and forth between tables, their destinations always clear to them. "Do you feel lost?"

"Right now?"

"No, like, all the time."

"Maybe some days." He studies me for a minute, his eyebrows drawn back down into a frown. "Is this because we don't have a permanent home?"

"A *real* home," I correct.

He sighs and leans back in the booth, keeping his hands on the table. The nail on his index finger has been bitten down to a nub. He does that when he's nervous. He must've done it when I left him and Nadia at the bus station earlier.

"Honestly, Jordie, even if we found a foster home to stay in for a while, I don't think it'd take that away. Finding a permanent home doesn't mean anything. We'll still remember the other ones."

"I know." I say it just because I don't want to argue with him again. The truth is, I think if we found our real family, then all the other stuff we've been through on earth wouldn't matter anymore. When we find the place we belong, none of the others will be important.

He shakes his head slightly and gives me a grin. "I really cannot believe I let you talk me into this."

I kick his shin under the table. "You're the one who said we should pack up and leave."

"Yeah, yeah." He kicks me back.

"You think Nadia will get in trouble?"

He shrugs. "She said she wouldn't. She's not a particularly great liar."

"I've noticed." I clear my throat and glance around to make sure Nadia and the waitress aren't near our table. "Do you remember Carl's dad?"

"Oh yeah." He shifts his gaze out the window, his grin dimming a little into a more wistful smile. "Remember he made you clean the baseboards with a toothbrush when he heard you cuss?"

"Yeah. And when he lost it on you and Carl that day he kicked us out."

He laughs slightly. "He lost his head over that stupid dare."

I study him for a second, trying to read his mind. I've never asked him about it because I didn't want him to feel bad, so he's never outright lied to me. "It's okay if it wasn't a dare."

"It was," he scoffs, crossing his arms over his chest.

"Okay. I'm just saying that if it wasn't, that's okay." I would never care if Joey liked kissing boys even when it wasn't a dare. He's my brother no matter what.

He opens his mouth, but before any words can come out, Nadia slides into the booth next to him. Joey clears his throat and looks at her. "Well? How much trouble are you in?"

"Oh, loads." She waves a hand before turning her phone screen on. "But that's not what I'm worried about."

She taps the screen twice, then lays the phone down on the table between me and Joey. A picture of the two of us stares up at me, with a headline over it that reads: TWINS MISSING FROM PAYSON, AZ.

"Oh, jeez." Joey sits back against the booth, his face paling.

"What're we supposed to do?" I ask. I think of the people who're out there searching for us because it's their job. Police officers and Camilla. Wasting time looking for people who aren't lost when they could be searching for ones who really need help.

"We'll call Camilla and let her know we're okay," Joey says decisively, like he read my mind.

I nod to show my support. Joey and I have done a lot of dumb things together, but never anything that could get someone hurt. At least not on purpose.

"Maybe wait until tonight," Nadia says. "She'll want you to go right back, and if you wait until tonight, at least you'll have tonight and tomorrow morning to stay here. I doubt Camilla would send someone out immediately. Right?"

"She would. We won't tell her where we are, but we'll let her know we're okay." Joey's chewing on his lower lip, which lets me know he's a lot more nervous about this than he's letting on. We have one of those moments where I swear I can read his mind. He's worried about whether or not Camilla will actually take us back if we do get in touch with her. We've been a lot of trouble, and Camilla has other kids to work with, kids that have a real shot at getting into permanent homes.

"It'll be all right," Nadia says bracingly. Then she looks at me with wide eyes, urging me to say something.

"Yeah, it'll be fine," I say. "I can call her if you want."

"Nah, it's okay. I got it."

I'm pretty sure he's only saying that because Nadia's with us. He doesn't like to look scared in front of anyone, not even me.

So I'll probably call her at some point tonight before Joey has to do it. But I'm not planning on telling her that we'll come back to Payson. We'll find answers in Roswell, answers that will lead us to our family, and then we'll never have to beg another person to take us in.

Calum's Guide to Extraterrestrials

I met with someone interesting today: a kid from Arizona who was looking into extraterrestrials. He's missing years of his life in memory, but what I found the most interesting were these marks on his back. This is his spine, and the circles are very similar to the ones from the "bull's-eye" rings in Arizona that were found twelve years ago.

I've seen scars on abductees before, usually small ones that can match up with medical instruments. I've never seen something like this before, not in person. Lots of people spend their lives waiting to see something like this up close. It's pretty irrefutable proof of an alien encounter. I commend this person for trying to find answers about what is obviously a confusing portion of his life.

The person I spoke to requested anonymity, so I won't name names, but he is a regular reader of the blog, so remember to always be kind when commenting or replying to comments.

TWENTY-TWO

I feel so sick to my stomach when I read Calum's newest blog post that I think I might throw up the burger I hoovered down back at the diner. Why did he post that picture after I asked him not to? Why did I let him take the photo in the first place?

The counter on the side of the website that shows how many hits the post is getting keeps rising. It's already up into the five figures.

God, if Camilla sees this . . . No, if Joey sees this, I'm dead. He hates this stuff. And I just got him to relax a little around it as we stay in Roswell for the day.

I clear the history on the phone and hand it back to Nadia.

"Everything okay?" she asks.

Numbly, I nod. It's not like I can give any different answer. I don't have a good enough lie to give them if I say I'm not okay.

Ahead of us, Joey huffs as he makes his way up the incline that'll lead us to Beth's house. Calum wasn't kidding when he said she lived near the quarry. It's like right on top of it.

By the time we finally reach it, even I'm feeling winded, and I run track at school. Nadia's sucking in deep breaths, her face and neck red.

Wordlessly, Joey hands her a bottle of water, then bends over with his hands braced on his knees.

"This is pathetic," I say, grabbing my own water bottle from the bag. "We look like we ran the Iron Man."

"Speak for yourself about being pathetic." Joey straightens up to poke my stomach. "You're the one who's supposed to be in shape."

I push the water bottle into his chest and move around him to jog up Beth's porch steps. While Alvin lived in a log cabin, Beth lives in a pretty white house with blue shutters and matching porch steps. There are flower boxes on the window-sill, and a privacy fence around the back of the house.

I knock twice, then take a step back in case she answers the door like Alvin does, with a pitchfork.

The person who opens the door is pitchfork-less, but a lot younger than I expected her to be. "Miss Beth?"

"No, I'm her caretaker, Donna. Are you from the youth group?"

"Um—"

"Yes," I interrupt Nadia before her honesty gets us kicked off the property. "We were hoping to talk to her."

"All right." She gives us a smile, tucks her red hair behind her ear, and widens the door for us to enter.

As soon as we step inside, I smell cookies baking. The warmth and sugar and butter are collecting in the air, and my stomach rumbles even though I'm not hungry.

"She's in the kitchen," Donna says. "I'll be in the living room. If you need me, just holler."

"Thank you," I say, but my attention is on the dark-skinned

woman at the table, carefully placing cookies into different tins. "Miss Beth?"

She looks up at the sound of my voice. "Oh, hello. You're a little early today."

I move closer to her, nerves shooting up all those marks on my spine. "Hi. I'm Jordie."

She gives me a bright smile. "Hello, Jordie. Oh, aren't you a little cutie."

My face heats while Joey coughs behind me. I don't know why he finds it so hilarious. We're identical; she thinks the same thing about him.

I rest my hands on the back of a wooden chair. "I was hoping we could talk to you for a minute."

"Well, sure, sweetie." She adds some more frosted sugar cookies to a tin.

"It's about the . . . UFO."

Her hands still and she looks up at me again, her eyebrows pulling together in confusion. "Why would you want to talk about that?"

"I'm hoping to find some answers, and anything you can tell me about that time would really help."

"Well, okay. I'm not sure I remember all of it, though. There are pieces of my time aboard the ship that I have no memory of."

I pull the chair out and sit across from her. "All you can tell me about it would be great."

She nods with a frown, closes one of the tins tightly with a lid, then moves on to the next one. "It was about ten years ago. I was out in the strawberry field down the road, when this horrible noise started up in the sky. I thought it was a helicopter at first, with a searchlight on. But the closer it got to earth, the more I realized it was a perfect circle. Couldn't have been more different from a helicopter."

Joey shifts behind me, but I ignore it. "What happened then?"

"A noise like an escalator starting happened. Then the light was all over me. It was so bright, I could barely see my hand in front of me." She holds her hand out to show me. "And then . . . then they pulled me up onto the ship."

"What was it like?" My voice is barely a whisper, the words getting stuck on the way out.

"Cold." She shivers. "So cold, child. And deathly quiet. There were lights everywhere. The bed spun under me, and I could see the red and blue lights spinning around me."

I swallow hard. It's just like what I remembered in my dream about Mom.

"Did you get a look at them?" Joey asks from behind me.

"Oh yes. Some looked just like how they're described on the big screen. They had great big green heads, long fingers. Big eyes. But others . . . well, they looked like you and me. I thought maybe they were other humans, except they had marks on them."

"What kind of marks?" I ask, my palms sweating so badly I have to wipe them on my jeans.

"Oh, they were circles, with little bits missing from the outer ones of the ring." She nods decisively. "The green ones didn't have those, but maybe I just didn't see because their skin was so different looking."

"Miss Beth, are you talking to these kids about those aliens?" Donna tsks as she enters the kitchen behind us. "You know you're not supposed to do that. It scares them."

Something shifts on my right. Joey again. I finally glance at him to see him staring at the screen of the laptop open on Beth's table. I glance back at Donna. "We asked her."

She gives me a smile and starts stacking the tins on top of one another. "You're not afraid of them?"

Before I can answer, Beth looks up, her gaze sharp and narrowed as she stares at me. "You're not afraid because you're one of them."

Nadia and Joey both stop moving. I think they stop breathing. I know I do.

"Miss Beth," Donna says, firmness entering her tone. "These are children from the youth center."

"No." She shakes her head before pointing at Nadia. "That one isn't an alien, but the other two . . . there's something not right about them. There's something in them." She licks her lips. "They're going to where the other aliens went in the desert. I can tell. They'll find the truth in the desert. They're looking—"

"Okay," Donna interrupts, and gives us an apologetic smile. "You know, I think maybe today's not a good day. You three should probably leave."

I open my mouth to protest, but Joey puts a hand on my shoulder, gripping almost painfully. So I stand and try to ignore Beth's eyes on me the entire time I move.

At the door, Donna gives us another smile, this one more sad than anything. "I'm sorry. This time of year always gets to her. It's when it happened."

"How long have you been working for her?" Nadia asks softly.

"Oh, about five years." She shakes her head. "She's been getting a little worse every year. But I've never heard her say something like that." She focuses on me and Joey. "Don't take it to heart."

"How do you know she's not telling the truth?" I ask.

Joey grips my elbow. "Of course she's not telling the truth. Let's go, Jordie."

"But—"

"Come on." He tugs on my arm. "Thanks for talking to us."

Donna waves at us from the porch as we start our way down the hill away from the quarry.

As soon as we get far enough away, Joey lets go of my arm.

"What's the matter with you?" I ask. "You said you'd be cool about this."

"Who did you talk to when you left us at the station?"

"What do you mean? I talked to Alvin with you."

"No, before that. You talked to someone who told you about Alvin and Beth. Who was it?"

I step back because his eyes are narrowing in suspicion. "What does it matter?"

"I saw a picture of you online, on the laptop Beth had open. It was a picture of one of the marks on your back."

All the spit in my mouth dries up. It hadn't even occurred

to me that other people in town would be looking at the blog. Or that Joey would see it. "I-I—"

"What were you thinking?" he demands. "We're trying to stay off the radar here, and whoever that was put it on his blog for everyone to see. If Camilla sees that, she'll know where we are."

"I told him not to put it on his blog." I shouldn't be defending myself. If he's mad at me, I deserve it. I knew it was a bad idea to let Calum take that picture.

"Why did you do that?" he asks. He's pleading now, as if that could take any of it back.

"Because I wanted his help."

"Did you meet that guy randomly in town?" Nadia asks, her voice full of skepticism. "Because it would seem to me that you'd have to talk to a lot of people before you found one who knew Alvin and Beth. And who happened to run a blog about aliens."

I shrink a little under her gaze. Then avoiding looking at either one of them, I admit, "I've been talking to him for a while online."

Joey makes a choked sort of noise and turns to start pacing the field. "You snuck away from us at the bus station so you could go meet some random guy you met online? What were you thinking, Jordie? You had no idea if he was who he said he was. You could've been meeting up with anyone."

"You think I hadn't thought of that?" I snap. "Joey, you're missing the bigger picture here. He was right. Alvin and Beth, they both know what they're talking about."

"Alvin, maybe." Joey stops pacing to turn and face me. "But Beth probably saw that picture online right before we got there. She described the marks too perfectly."

That is something I hadn't thought of.

Joey takes a breath and lets it out slowly. "Look, I'm not going back on my word. We're still going to look as much as we can while we can. But you have to stop doing stupid things, okay?"

I nod, even though I don't agree with him about Beth and the picture. Although . . . she did seem a little . . . off. Like she wasn't completely there when we were talking to her.

Joey shakes his head and starts walking again.

I start to follow him, but I only get one step in before Nadia taps the back of my hand to make me stop.

"Listen, Jordie." She runs her fingers along the knot in her suit jacket, still hanging from her waist. "Try to go a little easier on him."

"I said I was sorry about the photo. And the bus station thing." My stomach turns with guilt. "I don't know what else to do."

"It's not about that." She turns her head to make sure Joey's still a little ways away from us. "It's just . . . Joey doesn't want this. He doesn't want to be an alien and have been on a space-ship. He doesn't want the marks to mean anything. He wants them to be birthmarks."

"But they're not," I insist.

"I believe you. But it doesn't change the fact that it's not what Joey wants. He's doing all of this for you."

The guilt grows bigger, making me almost sick to my stomach. I hadn't looked at it that way. I knew Joey wasn't into it, but I thought it was because he didn't believe in it, not because he didn't want it to be true.

"Oh, jeez."

She tightens her suit jacket around her waist and then puts her hands on her hips. "Just try not to give him such a hard time, okay?"

"For the record, I never try to give him a hard time. Sometimes it just happens."

The corners of her mouth pull up in a smile. "Well. Still. Just think about it."

I nod to show her I will. I can't believe I never thought about that with Joey. I can usually read whatever's on his mind. It hadn't occurred to me that Joey would lock things away from me, like that time he kissed Carl. It scares me to think that there are other, bigger parts of Joey he's hiding.

Twenty-three

We're exhausted by the time we get back to town. None of us have really slept in twenty-four hours, but we can't afford a hotel room. And I don't think they'd let kids rent one anyway.

It's too hot outside to try sleeping out there. So Joey stops at a Walmart and we buy a few sets of earplugs. Then we go to the local theater and Joey buys tickets for the longest movie showing. Three hours total.

We take seats in the very back row, and my legs finally stop hurting. The previews haven't even started since we're about thirty minutes early to the showing. So we have the dark room all to ourselves.

Nadia sticks her earplugs in and immediately leans her head back against the seat.

Joey stretches his legs out in front of him and sighs. "We should've gotten some popcorn."

"We're supposed to be sleeping." I play with my earplugs instead of putting them in. "Listen, Joey, I'm really sorry about the picture thing. I really didn't think he was going to put it on his blog."

"It's okay." He rolls his earplugs across his thigh, back and forth. "It was just weird, you know? To see it online like that, where anyone could see. Even if no one could tell what the mark was even on."

"Do they embarrass you?"

"Yes." He doesn't hesitate before answering, which makes me think he's been feeling that way for a long time.

"Why?"

"I don't know." He shrugs and stares at the blank screen at the front of the room. "I guess it's because no one else has them. They're not normal."

"I think that makes them kind of cool."

That gets a smile out of him. "I guess I'm just a little worried about what will happen, what you'll do, if it turns out that we didn't come from aliens."

I frown. "What do you think I'll do?"

"I don't know." He goes back to rolling his earplugs. "Maybe you'll be mad at me."

"What? Why would I be mad at you? It's not like you know anything about them and are keeping it from me." I pause. "Right?"

"Yeah, I wouldn't do that. It's just . . . I feel like I should be able to help you more, and I can't."

"But don't you want this too?" I ask, staring at his profile.

"Of course I want this. I want a family. I'm just not as sure as you are that it's actually going to happen."

"Why not?" We've been through the same things. Does he really think so differently about it?

"I guess I just think that if it was going to happen, it would've happened by now. Camilla's been looking for years."

"Yeah, but if our DNA wasn't in the system already—"

"I know," he interrupts. "I just don't know if I can search forever, Jordie."

I sit back in my chair. I'd never thought of it like that. I could search forever. Isn't it worth it?

"The truth is, I'm not really sure what to do if this doesn't work out. I know you want to keep looking—"

"I won't without you," I cut him off. "If you want to go back, I'll go with you."

"Yeah?"

I feel bad that he even has to ask that. How could he not know I'd rather be with him? We're best friends. "Of course."

He smiles again, and some of the tension leaks out of his shoulders. Then he asks softly, "Did you mean what you said earlier? About not caring if the Carl thing wasn't a dare?"

"Of course I meant it."

He nods, then punches my shoulder. "Go to sleep. We still have to look at the ranch and then go to Area 51 when we wake up, then get a ticket for Nadia."

Without another word, he sticks his earplugs in and lays his head back.

I do the same, but I don't feel as relaxed as he does. The conversation we just had makes that ball in my stomach tighten even worse. Because I meant what I said about going home with him. This will be my only chance to find the truth about our family.

Twenty-four

When the movie's over, an usher wakes us up with a frown, telling us to exit the theater or buy more tickets to see the next showing.

We pocket our earplugs, then stagger out in the bright sunlight. My neck is pinched from how my head was when I slept, and my leg muscles are cramping. It feels good to get up and walk around.

Our bus is scheduled to leave in half an hour, so we head for the bus station and buy something to eat. Once we have our food, Joey hands Nadia some money. "That's for your ticket back to Payson once we're done at Area 51."

She slides it into her pocket. "What about you guys?"

"We don't know yet," Joey answers without looking at her. He's staring at the napkin dispenser. "We'll figure it out as we go along."

That hasn't exactly been working out for us too well so far, but what other choice do we have? We can't be separated.

"I don't really feel right, leaving you guys here alone while I go back home." Nadia's eyes are filled with guilt.

"It's okay," I say. It's not like we have a home to go to or anything. No one's waiting for us to come back. Well, maybe Camilla is, but that doesn't really count. She's only waiting for us so she can pass us on to another family. I don't blame her, it's her job, but she's getting paid to worry about us, which isn't the same.

But . . . I also don't want her thinking we were kidnapped by some crazed killer or something. So once Joey starts in on his hamburger, I tell him I have to go to the bathroom, and I slide out of the booth.

Just like at that diner when I called Nadia, I ask to use the phone behind the counter. The guy working it, Tony, is really nice and gives me the phone. And then a chocolate milkshake for free.

I smile my thanks as I dial Camilla's number. I'm not usually the one who calls her—it's usually Joey—so I mess up the numbers a couple times. But I get there in the end, and then I wait for the phone to ring.

It does it three times before she picks up. "Hello?"

I freeze at the sound of her voice. My palms start sweating. She must be so mad at us.

"Hello?" she repeats.

"Camilla? It's Jordie."

"Jordie?" Her voice rises. "Where are you? I've been worried sick."

"We're okay. I just wanted you to know we're safe. I'm sorry for making you worry." I hang up before she can say anything else. I feel guilty for making her scared, and guiltier for hanging up on her. But I don't want her to know where we are or where we're going. She'd try to talk me out of it, and I've come too far to let that happen.

I give the phone back to the guy behind the counter, then

take my milkshake with me back to the table where Joey and Nadia are sitting across from each other. I slide into the booth next to Joey and put the glass on the table.

Joey eyes it. "Where'd you get that from?"

"The guy behind the counter gave it to me."

"For free?" Nadia asks

I nod and take another sip of it.

"People do that sometimes," Joey says. "Once this guy who owned a candy store realized we were foster kids and gave us these huge bags of candy for free." His voice is starting to take on that dreamy quality it always has when he talks about candy.

"People seriously give you things just for being foster kids?" Nadia asks, her eyebrows drawn down in a frown.

Joey looks at her. "Well, we'd rather have a family."

She blushes. "O-Of course. I'm sorry. I didn't mean anything by it."

Joey grins. "Relax. I was messing with you." He checks the time on her phone that's lying on the table. "We have to leave in five minutes. Let me out, Jordie. I'm going to the bathroom."

I slide back out of the booth and wait for him to clamber out after me. Then I take my seat back and continue drinking my milkshake.

Nadia smooths her hair down and then tugs at the hem of her shirt. It's kind of funny to see her flustered like that. She's always so in control.

I turn my face away before she can see me smile.

"I really didn't mean anything by it," Nadia says when the

silence between us grows. "I wasn't trying to imply you were happy about your circumstances."

"Nadia, it's okay. Joey was just messing with you. He knew you weren't thinking that at all."

She huffs and tugs on her shirt again. "Then why would he say that?"

"I don't know. That's just how he does things." I drop my gaze and play with the cold, empty glass my milkshake was in. "It's just how he deals with stuff, you know? If he can joke about it, he can pretend nothing bothers him."

As soon as the words are out of my mouth, I want to cram them back in. Even though I'm sure Nadia's picked up on it because she's smart, it still feels like a betrayal to Joey, like I'm telling her something that was supposed to stay between us, even though we've never actually talked about it.

"Is that hard for you?" Nadia asks. Her voice has changed, turning softer.

"Maybe a little." I shrug. The truth is, I can't talk to her too much about it. Because he's my brother and I don't want to say anything bad about him. But sometimes it is super hard when he does this. I can talk to him about anything and I know he'll listen and understand in a way no one else ever could. But sometimes I wish he'd be a little more honest with me about how much being a foster kid bothers him.

I'm supposed to be the quieter one of the two of us, but sometimes Joey's silence is a lot louder than mine.

Twenty-Five

We walk to the bus station together. The sun's so hot, it makes me feel a little sick. I shouldn't have had that milkshake.

When we get on the bus, I realize Nadia's ticket is for a seat four rows back from ours. She sighs when she sees it, then says at least she got her phone charged enough to play games on.

As soon as she's gone, I sit next to Joey, who already snagged the window seat. He's tapping a rhythm on his thighs, almost nervously.

"You okay?" I ask.

"Mhmm." He nods for emphasis, but I can see the darkness circling in his eyes.

"Did what Nadia asked bother you?"

"What? No, of course not." He glances back to where she's sitting, frowning intently at her phone. "Why? Do you think she's upset? I was just joking around."

"She's not upset." I'm pretty sure she was a little, but I don't tell Joey that. I don't want him to feel bad.

He turns back to face the seats in front of us. "I'm just tired, Jordie. We've been traveling a long time and haven't really slept."

It's not the truth. I can hear it in his voice.

"Why do you do it?" I ask. "Joke around about that stuff? The fact that we're foster kids and have no real family."

Joey keeps his gaze set stubbornly on the seats. "What else am I supposed to do? I'm not like you, Jordie."

"What do you mean by that?"

"You know what I mean. I'm not good at thinking everything will be okay when it's pretty obvious it won't be."

I frown, thinking back on some of our conversations. "But you always tell me it'll be okay. And we don't lie to each other."

"No, we don't, and everything will be okay. Eventually. One day, we'll be eighteen and where we live won't be dependent on the state. But sometimes, the way we live really sucks, and I want to joke about it because it helps, okay?"

His voice has gotten rougher the longer he talked. He needs me to say it's okay. And it is. So I nod.

I'm not good at that stuff like he is. I can't joke about something that hurts. I find it kind of amazing that Joey can. "Thanks for telling me."

He huffs, but I can tell he's not actually angry. "You dragged it out of me. You're turning into Nadia."

"She's not so bad," I say.

"So you're saying you're glad she came with us."

"That's not even close to what I said." Honestly, I am glad she came with us. She helped us out when things got a little tough, and she wasn't that mad at me when I let our stuff get stolen all the way back in Las Cruces. Plus, she told Joey not to be mad at me about it. Even though I know he would've come around eventually and forgiven me, I think she pushed him to do it earlier than he planned.

Joey laughs and lays his head back against the seat. "Get

some more sleep. We only have a couple hours before we get to the ranch."

The J.B. Foster ranch sits on some sprawling land in Lincoln County, New Mexico. It's seventy-five miles outside of Roswell, but it's where the UFO of 1947 crash-landed. It's also currently in the process of changing owners.

We have to walk there from the bus stop, but it's not too far. Plus, it's pretty easy to spot from the road because it has a big sign on the property that boldly states it's the site of the UFO crash landing.

My heart starts pounding as soon as it comes into view. Roswell is known as the birthplace of aliens, but this is where it all started. I know if we had grandparents or something that landed here back then, they wouldn't still be here. They'd be in Area 51. But this is where it all started.

We come to a stop right at the property line. The grass is green and there are tire marks all through the dirt.

Joey takes a breath, his hands shoved deep into the pockets of his shorts. "I thought there'd be more tourists."

Nadia clears her throat and points to a sign that reads: Private Property. No Trespassing. Violators Will Be Prosecuted.

"Perfect."

I ignore them. But when I lift my foot to step onto the grass, Nadia grabs my arm. "It's a bad idea, Jordie."

"It's just for a second." I shake her off and plow ahead. I know there's nothing waiting there for me, not like in Roswell or what could be in Area 51. But I have to see it. This is important on a different level.

Joey and Nadia are silent, but I feel them following me. Nadia's too curious to stay behind, and I know that even if Joey doesn't want us to be related to aliens, he's curious too. What Alvin, and even Beth, said struck both of us.

We reach the exact site of the crash quicker than I expected. My legs are shaking and my arms are weights at my sides. I drag in a breath, tasting the soil and warmth on the air. It smells clean out here.

Nadia's looking around nervously, her hands fluttering around the jacket tied at her waist.

I stare down at the smooth dirt, imagining what it must've looked like in 1947, all jumbled and mashed from the UFO crash. I wonder if it had the same lights as the one that I was on when I was little.

A truck door slams somewhere to our right, and I jerk. Joey does the same next to me, then stands up on his toes to get a look at the vehicle.

"It's a truck," he says, his voice a whisper even though I'm pretty sure the person is too far away to hear anything we say.

"We should go," Nadia says. "We could get in a lot of trouble if we're caught."

"Yeah, I know." I take a small step back, but I don't want to look away from the spot. It sounds weird, but I can feel it pulling at me.

"Hey!" The voice comes from the same direction as the truck, and it sounds really, really angry.

"Come on." Joey grabs my arm, his fingers like a vise around my wrist.

I turn to follow him when I see it. There in the dirt is half a circle. It looks almost exactly like the ones on our spines, but only half of it. "Look," I say, pointing with my free hand.

Joey spares it a glance, then takes a longer second look. "Okay. That's a little freakish."

Nadia glances once in the direction of the guy approaching, then moves in for a closer look at the half circle. "That's weird. It looks fresh."

"Our blood will be too if we don't get out of here." Joey tugs on my wrist again. "Let's go."

Nadia pauses to snap a picture of the mark, and then we turn and run for the sign where we entered the property.

Twigs snap behind us, but it's too far away for me to properly worry.

We don't stop running even when we reach the sign. We fly by it and continue up the road until the ranch looks like a speck in the distance. When we stop, Joey lets go of my arm and braces his hands on his knees, sucking in air just like he did after that hike to Beth's house.

Nadia puts her hands on her hips and looks up at the sky, as if doing that will help the air fill her lungs faster.

I have a stitch in my side and my chest feels like it's going to collapse.

"Tell me you got a good picture," Joey says.

Nadia pulls her phone back out and hands it to him. I look

over his shoulder at it. It *is* a good picture. The lines are clearly defined, and she was right; they look fresh.

"It could be from a tool or something," Joey says, the slightest hint of disbelief creeping into his voice.

Irritation licks at me, but I push it away. Just because I believe in them doesn't mean Joey has to.

But it would make this whole thing smoother.

"It's pretty close to what's on your backs, even if it's not an exact match," Nadia says, using her fingers to zoom in closer on the photo.

"We could go back and ask that guy about it," I say.

Joey cuts me a glare. "You better be kidding."

I shrug. Because I kind of am, but I'm also kind of not.

"I'm pretty sure he had a gun," Nadia says. "So I'm with Joey on the not going back thing."

The disappointment must show on my face, because Joey's gaze softens. "Hey, you heard what Alvin said. After it left the ranch, after Roswell, it went to Area 51. If there's anything to find, it'll be there, okay?"

I nod, even though I want to go back and keep looking. But Joey's right. Hanging around the place where they once were won't help me reach them. And right now, finding them matters the most.

TWENTY-SIX

The white light blinds me. I'm so hot all over. It feels like my skin is on fire. I raise my hands, trying to scratch it off.

"Shh." Someone leans over me, the head so large it blocks the bright light. "You're okay, Jordie."

I close my eyes again because even with her blocking out the light, it still hurts to look at it. Everything hurts. "Mom?"

The woman squeezes my hand in response. It's her.

"We have to get them to safety," she says, her voice full of command and urgency.

I try to open my eyes, to get a better look at her, but the lights are starting to spin in a circle. They're different colors now, blue and green. The floor's moving.

Long, rubbery fingers grip my wrist.

"We have to send him now," the woman says. "He needs to go."

I wake with a gasp when Joey shakes my arm. And then frustration pours into me. I was so close that time. So close to seeing the place I was in with my mom. My lungs are aching again like they did on the bus when I had this dream, and I can already feel it slipping away from me again.

"What's up?" Joey asks.

"Nothing." I straighten my T-shirt, which is starting to

smell like I've had it on for over twenty-four hours. Then I wipe my chin to make sure there's no drool.

"Come on. The bus is stopping. We can't get any closer to Area 51 on it. We have to start walking."

I stagger up from the seat and blink to clear the remaining sleep from my eyes. Behind us, Nadia covers her mouth with her hand as she yawns. Joey's the only one who looks wide awake. And he's watching me.

"What?" I finally ask.

"What were you dreaming about?"

"That thing I already told you." For some reason, I don't want Nadia hearing this, and I don't know why. She's helped us through everything else. But this just feels more personal, closer to just me and Joey.

"Was it the same as last time?" Joey asks quietly, falling in line behind an old guy as we make our way slowly toward the front of the bus.

"Yeah. But I think if you hadn't woken me, I would've remembered more." I hitch our bag higher up on my shoulder. "I need to sleep, really sleep, and maybe it'll come back in full."

"Maybe," Joey says, but he doesn't sound sure.

"Don't you want to dream about her too?" I ask, keeping my voice low.

"No." Joey's answer is swift and certain. "I don't want to dream about someone who abandoned us in a field."

"But maybe—"

"Jordie." He looks back at me. "Alien or not, she left us. They left us."

"Yeah, but maybe they didn't want to. You don't know."

He gives me an even look, and I think there's a bit of pity in his eyes. But then he turns his face back to the door of the bus. "We'll see."

We step off the bus, and I breathe in the fresh air. It's still pretty hot out, even though it's already dark. And the air smells different here, like it has smoke in it or something. It's different from the air in Payson.

Nadia brings up the map on her phone, and we start off in the right direction.

"It's going to be a little tough," Nadia admits. "Area 51 isn't exactly on maps, because it's a military base. So you guys are just going to have to trust me. And maybe not get too mad if I lead us wrong a couple times."

Joey looks over her shoulder at the phone. "Well, we've got six hours until we have to get you to Vegas to catch the bus to Payson. We promise not to yell."

She nods absentmindedly, then quickens her pace the farther we get from the bus station.

My limbs are full of tension and anticipation. I've thought about Area 51 for a long time, ever since I started thinking that Joey and I had come from outer space. It feels weird to be going there, to this place I've had in my mind for so long.

But I'm right. I know I'm right. They're in there somewhere. They have to be. And once we find them, we can leave the foster system and finally have a real family and a real home. We won't have to worry about being separated anymore.

The three of us walk silently through the streets of Rachel,

Nevada, and I'm thankful we got here when we did. I don't think I could've walked in the daylight again. My skin is painful from my sunburn, and I can see it on Joey's face and neck. It's on Nadia's nose. Like really badly.

She notices me looking and gives me a grim smile. "Our chances of developing skin cancer later in life have gone up a considerable percentage over the last two days."

That . . . wasn't exactly something I wanted to hear.

Joey grunts. "Maybe if Jordie and I aren't actually humans, we can't get skin cancer."

"That's a fair point," she says with a nod. "Maybe you can't experience puberty either."

"There wasn't a need for that." Joey scowls. "Aliens probably turn out way better than human guys after puberty."

"Maybe. There are a lot of people obsessed with aliens. It could actually be great for your love life when you get older."

My nose wrinkles before I can stop it. My love life isn't something I'm concerned about right now.

She laughs when she catches the look on my face. "Relax, Jordie. You will be much, much older before that happens, okay?"

Joey smirks and bumps my shoulder with his. "I don't think Jordie will be *too* much older when that starts."

My face heats even though I don't want it to. I know he's talking about Nadia. Does she know? God, I hope not. That would be mortifying. Also, what person our age uses the phrase "love life"?

Fortunately, before either one of them can say anything

else, there's a low whine from down one of the side streets on our right.

My heart clenches, and I pause. It sounds just like a dog I knew a few years ago. Rocky. He belonged to one of the foster couples Joey and I stayed with when we were nine. The foster dad used to kick Rocky whenever he was angry. The foster mom would always ask him not to, but it never changed. When Joey and I were moved to a new foster home, we asked Camilla to take Rocky away from that family. I don't know if she did or not. She never told us.

I turn and run down the side street, following the sound of the dog. His whine is growing louder, and more pained. Then I see him, huddled behind a dumpster. He has no collar or tag, and he's pretty dirty.

Underneath the grime, I can tell he's a terrier of some kind. He's shivering and so, so tiny.

As soon as I reach him, I hold out a hand, but he shies away from me, pulling deeper into the corner of the alley. So I lower myself down to my knees, trying to ignore the way the gravel bites into them. It makes me look smaller, and less threatening to him.

He paws at the ground nervously.

I try again to hold out a hand, and this time he sniffs my fingers tentatively. His nose is wet and it tickles my skin, but I don't move. I don't want to scare him away.

That gets ruined when Joey and Nadia appear behind me, huffing like they ran a marathon.

The dog pulls back immediately with a whimper.

"Oh," Joey says softly. "Oh no."

"I think he's hungry," I say. "Can you get him something to eat?"

"Yeah, yeah." I feel Joey shift behind me. "Just stay right here though, okay?"

"I will." I'm already reaching for the dog again when my brother turns to leave.

Nadia stays, and eventually, she squats next to me. The dog is already back out, sniffing my fingers again. Then he gives my hand a cautious lick and moves closer to me.

"You're good at this," Nadia whispers. "Have you had a dog before?"

I shake my head but start telling her about Rocky. It's the first time I've talked about him since Joey and I told Camilla. The few times Joey tried to bring it up, I wouldn't say anything. Even now, just thinking about him makes me want to cry.

When I'm done telling Nadia—fortunately not having cried through it—she stares at me for a long few minutes. The silence is so loud that I want to pull away from her. But that would mean pulling back from the dog, who's currently scooting closer to me little by little.

Nadia finally shakes her head. "I've heard of stuff like that, but I've never known anyone who's actually seen it."

I stay silent while the dog slowly lays his head on my thigh. I keep stroking his fur even though it's matted. I try not to snag on any of the tangles because it'll hurt him.

"I'm sorry you had to see that," Nadia says softly.

"It's okay."

"No, I'm really sorry. Your lives . . . they've been so challenging. It's no wonder you're so determined to find your family."

"I can't go to another foster home," I mumble, running my fingers through the dog's fur so I don't have to concentrate on the stinging in my eyes. "And I can't be without Joey."

She nods, and I think she understands even though she's never been in my place. Nadia cares, even if it doesn't affect her.

Joey reappears behind us suddenly, out of breath again. He's already prying open cans of wet dog food.

I take one from him and set it on the asphalt next to me, using my hand in the dog's fur to guide him closer.

Just like when he licked my hand earlier, he tentatively starts eating. He pauses to look up at us every few seconds, like he's waiting for one of us to take it away from him. I keep a hand on his back so he knows I'm not moving. Then I try really hard to swallow around the hard lump in my throat. I'll never understand how someone could do this to an animal.

Joey kneels slowly on my other side. The dog tenses under my hand, but returns to eating, going a little faster now.

What makes this worse is the dog reminds me of Joey and me. He has no home and no family and no one willing to take care of him.

"We should take him with us," I say, the words barely making it out because my throat's so tight. Images of Rocky keep flashing in my mind.

"He might belong to someone," Nadia points out softly.

"It doesn't matter," Joey says. "He's coming with us. If he

does belong to someone, that person's obviously horrible. We're not leaving him here."

"Okay." Nadia raises her hand in the gesture of surrender. "Give him another can of food. Poor thing's starving."

Joey pops the top off a second can, and I take it from him, placing it right next to the first one. The dog moves to it, a little less cautiously than he went at the first one.

"You should name him," Joey says.

I think for a minute, going over everything we've done on this trip, what brought us here to finding the dog.

Joey looks at me, and we have one of those seconds where I swear I can read his mind, and I don't know if it's alien genes or just a twin thing. But we both say, "Roswell."

Nadia grins. "That's perfect."

As soon as Roswell finishes the second can of food, I start scratching behind his ears, then cooing his new name to him until I'm sure he'll come if I call him it.

Joey gathers the now empty cans and tosses them into the dumpster. He still has three more cans of food in the plastic bag dangling from his wrist.

Once I'm sure Roswell will stay with us, I stand. He does the same, straightening up onto all fours, his ears perked up. His tail wags fiercely behind him.

"Come on, boy," I say, and as soon as I step forward, Roswell does the same. Then the four of us start again in the direction of my family.

TWENTY-SEVEN

Roswell's a good dog. He stops to sniff things along the way, but never slows us down. Which is good because stopping to feed him and get him to trust me took thirty minutes away from our time to get to Area 51. But that's okay. I'm glad we stopped.

We get turned around twice, and Nadia sighs both times in frustration before turning us back the right way.

We walk for an hour, and just when I think we're lost again, she starts pointing excitedly. "It's there! Right there!"

Her raised voice makes Roswell shy against my legs, so I shush Nadia and reach down to pet the dog.

"Sorry." Even her whispered apology comes out excited. "I just can't believe we found it." She checks the time on her watch. "But I only have a couple hours before I have to start back for the bus station."

We start jogging in the direction of Area 51. In the distance I can just make out several tall power lines, and a large blockade at the front.

As we get closer, I realize the blockade is one of those black-and-white striped bars that lowers to keep cars from driving onto the base. There's a big stop sign on the front of the bar.

Joey hesitates, looking around the area. "Jordie, I-I don't know about this."

I stop, my shoes skidding just a little on the dirt road. Roswell nudges the back of my leg with his head. "What do you mean? You promised you'd see this through."

He looks around the area again. "Do you know how much trouble we could get in if someone finds us?"

"It'll be worth it." I make my voice as firm as I can. I can't have him bow out now. Not after we've come so far.

Nadia glances between the two of us but stays silent. Still, I feel the impatience rolling off her. She wants to know what's behind there almost as much as I do.

"Okay," Joey relents. "Okay but be careful. We have to stick together."

I nod immediately, anything to get us beyond this barrier and actually onto the base.

Joey takes a huge breath, then ducks under the gate without warning. I scramble to follow, and I feel Roswell right at my side. Nadia's behind me. As soon as we cross onto the base, she grabs my hand. It's clammy, but I don't know if it's from fear or anticipation.

We've barely gotten five steps in when a massive floodlight turns on directly over us.

Nadia squeals and tightens her hold on my hand.

Joey starts running in the opposite direction, so I follow him. Roswell runs along beside us, his paws hitting the ground quieter than our sneakers.

Nadia's panting behind me, and Joey's weaving back and forth, as if he's afraid we're about to get shot. He keeps glancing back to make sure we're following him.

My fingers are starting to hurt from how tightly Nadia's clutching them. And then I hear metal on metal, like a gate opening.

"Stop!" The voice rings out like a gunshot, and my heart starts jackhammering in my chest. They're going to catch us. I can feel it.

The spotlight swings around, blinding me. I stumble over the ground, nearly dragging Nadia down with me.

Another sound fills the air, like a popping. And I know from watching a million TV shows that the sound is a gun being cocked.

The three of us freeze. My lungs ache, and my stomach is convulsing. I think I'm going to hurl.

Roswell paces nervously in front of me, but he's not whining like he was in the alley. He's growling now, at the men slowly approaching with their guns aimed right at us.

Twenty-eight

The spotlight's so bright that I want to bring a hand up to shield my eyes, but I'm afraid the soldiers are going to shoot me if I move a muscle.

My heartbeat's pounding in my ears, and I can't seem to let go of Nadia's hand.

Joey slowly reaches back, grabbing onto my free wrist.

The soldier closest to us frowns. "Are you kids aware you're on a US military base without clearance?"

My knees are knocking together so hard, I swear the soldiers around us must be able to hear them.

"We're sorry," Joey says, his voice loud but wavering. "It was an accident. We'll leave right now."

"No." I don't even realize I'm stepping forward until I almost trip over Roswell. "No, we can't leave."

"Jordie." Joey snaps my name like it's a bad word. "We're going."

I shake his hand off. "We're not leaving. Not until we find our parents."

The soldier in the front lowers his gun, his brows knitting together in confusion. "Your parents? Do they work on the base? We can radio them if there's an emergency."

"No, there's no emergency," Joey says, his words tripping

over each other in their rush to get out. "We're sorry we bothered you."

"Joey." I glare at him, and there's no way he can miss it in all the brightness coming from the floodlight. Why is he doing this? "We came all this way."

Joey stays stubbornly silent, his eyes narrowed in anger and fear.

"Okay," the soldier in front of us says. "Look, you kids are already in trouble for sneaking onto the base. If you want us to call your parents for you—"

"Yes," I say before Joey can speak. "But they don't work here. They . . . stayed here."

How else am I supposed to say they were taken captive by the government when they crash-landed?

"When?" the soldier asks.

"Jordie, stop." Joey sounds so close to crying that I listen to him. I haven't heard him sound like that in a long time.

"Joey, we have to—"

"They're not here. They were never here."

Frustration zips through my veins, making me curl my hands into fists. "I know you don't believe in this, but—"

"I don't believe in it because I already know that it's not true," Joey yells. Twin patches of red appear on his cheeks as he stares at me. "Those marks on our spines aren't from an alien race. We got them when we were seven."

"What are you talking about?"

"It was our foster mom, Melinda. She held a cigarette lighter to our backs just to hear us scream."

I jerk back, as if it can stop my ears from hearing his words. "No." I shake my head. "The field . . ."

"We weren't left there by a ship. Regular human parents left us there because they didn't want us. We're not aliens. We're just garbage. That's what people do with garbage. They throw it away."

Beside me, Nadia gasps sharply. In front of me, Roswell paces nervously, picking up on my fear and anger and disbelief. And the fact that the disbelief is turning into belief. Because it makes more sense. Even now, I feel the phantom pains of the cigarette lighter on my skin. I remember hearing Joey scream.

Still, I shake my head. I don't want it to be true. It can't be. Joey went along on this whole thing, and he wouldn't have done that if he'd known the truth.

"Jordie." Joey takes a step toward me, but I move away. I let go of Nadia's hand, then I turn and run in the direction we came from. Past the blockades and orange traffic cones, back under the striped gate to keep vehicles out. Past the fence and stone pillars on either side. All the way out onto the dirt road.

I don't know if the soldiers will follow me, and I don't care if they do. I just need to get away.

Roswell keeps pace right next to me as I run. It helps to hear his paws hitting the ground in the same rhythm as my feet, but it doesn't take any of it away.

As soon as I clear the dirt road, I head back for the tiny town that led us here. Its lights are glowing in the distance, and I know if I keep my head down and run, I can reach it quickly.

There's shouting behind me, but they're so far back already

that there's no way they'll reach me. Besides, it doesn't sound like Nadia, who's the only one I could really talk to right now. For once, I can't stand the thought of talking to Joey.

I suck in a breath, ignoring the stitch in my side, and put on more speed.

How could Joey have not told me this? And how could I have forgotten it in the first place? How could five years pass without me realizing what had really happened?

I cut down the first alley I see. There's a dumpster off on the right side, and it reminds me of what Joey said. About us being garbage.

As soon as his face flashes into my head, I stumble. I veer to the left so I don't hit Roswell, then I'm falling, landing on my bare knees on the asphalt. It stings my skin, and I feel it split open, but I can't bring myself to care.

My head pounds. The memory is coming.

Joey crying and screaming. Joey begging our foster mom to *please, please* stop. The sizzling noise the lighter made when it touched my skin. The burning that lasted for days. Camilla looking at us with tears in her eyes. Me asking her if we could go to a new home now. Days spent in the hospital.

My stomach convulses and I lean up on all fours and hurl what's left in my stomach out onto the street. It really happened. We don't have parents waiting for us anywhere. They really never wanted us. No one's ever wanted us.

I wipe my mouth with the back of my hand and try not to cry. But I keep seeing the look on Joey's face when he yelled at me back in Area 51. No wonder he fought me so much about the aliens. This is why he wasn't willing to look until he knew we were going to be separated. Because there's really nothing for us. We had human parents who left us in a field for dead. We're lucky to be alive.

I close my eyes, and Roswell nudges my hand with his wet nose, checking on me. I lift that hand and place it on his back, stroking his fur gently, keeping my eyes closed.

Now that the memory of the burns is actually in my mind, I can see more. The dreams I've been having, they were real. But the woman who was talking wasn't my mom, it was an EMT. She was the one holding my hand. The flashing lights were the police cars. The constant moving was from the ambulance I rode in the back of as they took me to the hospital. I remember asking them over and over if Joey was okay.

I sniff and bury my face in Roswell's fur. I don't even care that it's still matted. He stands still when I circle my arms around his neck and hold on to him. I wish more humans were like dogs. Roswell already likes me and all I did was feed him and be nice to him.

"What am I supposed to do now?" I whisper. "When we go back to Payson, they're going to split us up. And we'll never have a real home because we don't have a real family waiting for us. We never did."

Roswell can't answer, but he puts a paw on my thigh, like he understands.

"I don't know how I'm supposed to go into another home without Joey." Even though I'm angry with him for lying to me, and keeping that a secret for so long, it doesn't make me want to be away from him. I need him. And I realize that he needs me more than I ever thought before.

My hands shake on Roswell's fur as I think back to everything that happened over the last few days that brought me here. Nadia and Calum and Alvin and Beth. Beth turned out to be right. I did find the truth in the desert.

I stay like that for a long time, hugging Roswell close to me. Until a throat clears uncertainly behind me.

I wipe my eyes quickly, then turn to face the woman at the opening of the alley. There's a man standing next to her in a baseball cap, glancing around uncomfortably.

"Hey." The woman approaches me slowly before squatting so she's eye level with me like a lot of adults do. "Do you need help?"

I swallow hard, keeping my grip tight on Roswell. "I'm lost." It's the first time I've ever said those words, but I realize I've been lost all my life. And the reason I haven't been found is because there's no one out there looking for me.

Her eyes soften. "You need help finding your parents?"

"I don't have any." The words are raw coming up from my throat. I must have them out there somewhere, but it doesn't matter.

"Oh." It slips out of her mouth like a gasp, except quieter. "Well, we can take you to the police station. It's just a little ways down the street."

I run my hand over Roswell's back, thinking. I need to get back to Area 51, back to Joey and Nadia. But there's no way I'd be able to find that place by myself. I hadn't been paying attention on the way there because I didn't think I'd need to go back.

"Yeah," I finally say. "That sounds okay."

If I talk to the police, I might be able to find Joey and Nadia. I'm sure the military would talk to them. Even if we are in a lot of trouble for sneaking onto the base. I remember the big guns the soldiers had, and I shiver.

The lady takes my hand and pulls me up from the ground, then brushes the shoulders of my shirt off. "Come on." She gives me a soft smile. "Let's get you to the station."

TWENTY-NINE

I walk between them, Roswell never leaving my side as we cross the street. I can see the lights of the police station already, and it reminds me of my memory. The one of the EMT in the ambulance, the flashing lights.

When we get to the station, I'm surprised when the man and woman walk in there with me. I'm sure I'm not supposed to bring animals in here too, but I don't leave Roswell outside. I can't do that.

As soon as we're inside, the lady heads for the front desk, where a young cop is busy stapling something together. He looks up at us with a smile. "What can I do for you guys?"

"We found him in the alley," the woman says in a whisper, like she's worried I'm going to overhear. "He says he's lost and doesn't have parents."

The cop turns to me, his smile dimming slightly. "What's your name?"

"Jordie."

The cop nods, asks the couple a few questions about where they found me, and then he says they can go.

The guy steps forward slightly and leans over the desk. "His knees are all busted up. I think he may have fallen. Can you make sure someone takes care of those for him?"

"Yeah, yeah, definitely." The cop waits until the couple

turns to leave before looking back at me. "All right, Jordie. Come with me."

I follow him down a long hallway and into a private room.

"Go ahead and take a seat," he says, indicating a chair in the corner. "I'm Officer Dean. We've been hoping you'd show up."

I blink to clear my mind. "You have?"

"Yep. A couple officers brought in your brother and friend about half an hour ago." He opens a cabinet, then looks back at me. "You guys caused quite the stir sneaking onto that base."

I lower my head, remembering the way the soldiers surrounded us. The way they held their guns. "I think they were going to shoot us."

Officer Dean pulls a white first aid kit off a shelf, then closes the cabinet doors. "They were pretty understanding once your brother told them the whole story."

"Are we in actual trouble? Like with the law?" That was something that hadn't occurred to me until I heard Joey and Nadia were here too. I guess I'd never really considered getting into trouble for being on the base.

"No. But we did get in touch with your caseworker, and we'll be sending you back to Payson as soon as this is all cleared up."

My throat tightens, and I look away from him before I start crying again. Back to Payson. That means Joey and I will be separated. Roswell whines beside me.

Officer Dean kneels in front of me and opens the first aid kit. "How'd you get these?"

"I fell in the alley," I reply, my voice barely louder than a whisper. "I tripped."

He rips open some alcohol wipes. "This is going to hurt a little bit."

I nod for him to keep going. I don't even care.

He cleans them, and it does sting, but it feels okay. It helps me snap out of it a little more.

"So, what's your dog's name?" Officer Dean asks.

"Roswell." The word scratches my throat. I want to go find Joey and Nadia. I want to get out of here.

"That's a cool name," Officer Dean says with a nod, and I can tell he's saying it because he really believes it, not just because he thinks I want to hear it.

I reach out and lay my hand on Roswell's head. He responds by laying his head on my thigh, his ears close to Officer Dean's hands.

"When can I see my brother?"

"As soon as I get you fixed up. The captain wants to talk to you, and then he'll take you to see your brother and friend."

"What's he want to talk to me about?"

"Not sneaking onto military bases." He opens two large Band-Aids and presses them gently to my knees. "Feel better?"

I nod. "Thank you."

"Sure." He snaps the kit closed and puts it back in the cabinet. "I'll go get the captain. Hang out in here, okay?"

I nod again, and he disappears out the door.

As soon as he's gone, Roswell perks back up, his tail wagging. It almost makes me smile.

A large man steps into the doorway. He has gray hair and bushy eyebrows. He also has a really thick mustache. But his eyes are kind and understanding. "Hello, Jordie. It's nice to meet you. You've given everyone here quite a scare."

"I'm sorry." Then I frown. "Why?"

"We weren't sure what had happened to you. Military personnel showed up on our doorstep, and that's not exactly a common occurrence. And your brother and friend were pretty out of their minds with worry. They thought maybe you'd run off permanently."

I look away from him. "I wouldn't do that to Joey."

The captain drags a chair out from the other corner and pulls it over to me. He turns it so it's facing me, then sits in it. "You realize how much trouble the three of you could be in for sneaking onto a military base?"

I swallow hard. "It was my idea. Please don't punish my brother or Nadia."

"No one's getting punished," he says. "You're all getting warnings to never, ever do it again. If you do, there'll be consequences. You understand?"

I nod so hard it hurts my neck. I don't care if I get in trouble; we're probably already in a world of it with Camilla. But I do care if Joey and Nadia get hurt because I was dumb enough to think we were somehow related to aliens. They could've gotten sent to jail because of me.

"Officer Dean told you someone's on their way to pick you up?"

"Yes, sir."

"Do you have any other questions?"

I start to shake my head, then change my mind. "Can I get my dog some water?"

"Sure. Come with me and we'll get him something to drink."

I stand from the chair, trying not to wince when it causes pain to shoot up my knees. I barely remember falling.

The captain takes me to a conference room, where Joey and Nadia are, and then he disappears to get Roswell some water.

Joey's slouched in a chair in the corner of the room, his head in his hands. Nadia's standing by the large table, facing a man who looks a lot older than her. He has his hands on her upper arms, but he's not angry.

"Anything could've happened to you," he's saying, the words shooting out of his mouth quickly. "You could've been hurt or kidnapped or killed."

"I know, Papa. I'm so sorry." Nadia glances at the door, and when she realizes I'm there, her eyes light up with relief. She pries her dad's hands off her arms. "We can go home, Papa. You can ground me forever."

He reaches for her again, but she ducks away from him and lunges at me. She wraps her arms around me, squeezing tightly. "Jordie, I'm so glad you're okay. Joey and I were so worried about you."

When Joey hears my name, his head snaps up, and he stares at me. His eyes are rimmed with red, and there are pink splotches on his cheeks. He looks as miserable as I feel.

Nadia pulls away, and I get a good look at her. She has smudges of dirt on her face and shirt. Her suit jacket is long gone. There's dust and mud on the tops of her once-white flats. "My papa is taking me home, but I'll see you in school, okay?" Then she leans in close, her mouth near my ear. "I'm so sorry about what happened, Jordie. About Area 51 and Joey keeping the truth from you, and what happened when you guys were little. And I'm really glad you're back."

When she pulls away again, I give her a smile. I tell her I'll see her at school, though from the look on her father's face, I'm guessing he doesn't necessarily want us hanging out together.

As soon as they leave, the captain reappears with a bowl and a water bottle. He opens the bottle and pours it into the bowl, then sets it in front of Roswell. The dog looks up at me first, like he's making sure it's okay with me if he drinks.

I nod and he seems to understand me because he leaves my side and trots over to the bowl.

"Here," the captain says, handing me two bottles of apple juice and two packages of crackers. "The agent coming to pick you up will be here in about an hour. Let me know if you guys need anything more to eat, okay?"

"Okay. Thank you."

He gives me a smile, then leaves the room, closing the door behind him.

Slowly I make my way over to Joey and hand him one of the bottles and packages of crackers. The plastic crinkles when it changes hands. The bottle leaves cold condensation on my fingertips.

I sit in the chair next to him and balance my bottle of juice on my leg.

Joey doesn't open his. "I didn't think you were coming back."

"What? Why wouldn't I?" It had never occurred to me to stay gone. Joey's my best friend. I can't be without him.

"Because I lied to you all that time. I knew it was a mistake to come here, and even going to Roswell in the first place."

"Then why did you?"

"Because I didn't know what else to do." His shoulders slump. "I don't want to be separated."

"Me neither." I stare at the package of crackers in my hand, then eventually just open the juice bottle. I drain the whole thing in a few gulps. Then I ask him the question that's been weighing on me since I left Area 51. "Why didn't you just tell me about all of that? Why did you let me keep believing we were related to aliens because of the marks?"

"The doctor told us it would be better if you remembered on your own," Joey says softly. "He said you would eventually."

I stay silent, staring down at the empty juice bottle. How could I have forgotten something like that? Especially since I can remember it so clearly right now. I can even remember the smell of my skin after it burned. It was horrible.

"I'm really sorry," Joey whispers. "I shouldn't have told you. Or . . . maybe I shouldn't have kept it from you in the first place."

I look over at him, watch the way his shoulders move as he breathes. "I don't think we're garbage."

He looks up. "I shouldn't have said that."

"Do you think it's true?"

He shrugs. He always does that when I ask something he doesn't want to answer.

"Joey," I press.

"I don't know," he finally admits. "Part of the reason why I agreed about going to Roswell was because if we were searching for them, I could pretend they were really out there looking for us. But they're not."

Roswell comes back to me, probably sensing how exhausted I am. He rests his body on my sneaker and presses his back against my leg, offering me his warmth.

"It's okay if we never find them," I say, looking at Joey. "Remember that game we used to play, when we would imagine all the things we'd do with our parents if they came back for us?"

Joey nods, a quick jerk of his head that tells me he's still really sad.

"We can still do all those things, even if we don't have parents. We can still travel and graduate and celebrate birthdays. You've been my only family for a long time, and it's been all I've needed so far."

He swallows hard and then looks up at me, studying my eyes. "You really mean that?"

"Yeah. I'll always wish we had parents, Joey, but if we don't find them, I'll be okay. We'll both be okay."

He takes a deep breath, then lets it out slowly. His hands are shaking, but I think my words made him feel better. We're all each other has had for our whole lives. Not even Camilla counts because she hasn't been there with us through every house. She's planted us in them and left. And I know it's her job, and I'm thankful she's kept us together for so long, but she still wasn't there.

It was me and Joey who stole things with Henry. It was me and Joey who watched Rocky get kicked over and over. It was me and Joey who were shoved out of the house after Joey and Carl kissed. It was me and Joey getting burned together in matching circles. It was me and Joey all the way back, twelve years ago, left in a field alone.

"We will be okay," Joey says, repeating my words with more confidence. Then he gives me a smile. "I'm glad you're back. Nadia kind of lost her mind, she was so worried about you. Oh, and her dad hates us both."

"Yeah, I kind of picked up on that from the way he glared at me when I came in here."

"You missed the whole speech. He ranted about how we corrupted her because his 'good little girl' would never do something like this on her own."

"Did that make Nadia mad?"

"Oh yeah. Then they got into this whole conversation about legal rights and I could only follow half of that." He opens his package of crackers and starts eating. "Apparently he got here so quickly because he was already on his way. He'd started tracking her cell phone a few hours ago when he couldn't get ahold of her."

I frown, opening up my own package. "You'd think she would've thought of that."

"Yeah. She was pretty disappointed in herself, I could tell." He shrugs, then says, "She's a good friend."

"Yeah. She is."

We eat in silence for a little while, and Joey gives me some of his juice when the dry crackers almost make me choke. And before long, the door opens again, and Officer Dean reappears.

"Boys? It's time to go home."

THIRTY

Officer Dean walks us out to the lobby, where a guy in black pants and a white dress shirt is waiting for us. He's yawning behind his hand, and I feel a sudden surge of guilt in my stomach. He probably hasn't slept, and was sent here to come pick us up.

"Hey, kids," the guy says, then surprises me by reaching out to shake our hands. His is strong, and mine disappears inside it. "I'm Connor. I'm taking you guys back to Payson, okay?"

I nod. It's not like we have much of a choice in the matter.

Connor holds his hand out to Roswell too, letting him sniff it.

"You guys need anything else?" Officer Dean asks, handing me the small bag we had Roswell's food crammed in.

"No. Thank you though," I say.

He gives us a smile, and then a wave as we set off out the doors with Connor. He opens the back door of the white car for us, then shuts it as soon as we're inside.

When he climbs into the front seat, he turns the ignition and the car roars to life. "Well, we've got a five-hour drive ahead of us. You guys need something to eat? You must be starving."

I look over at Joey, and he shrugs. "Okay."

Connor drives for a few minutes before pulling off the

road and into the parking lot of a McDonald's. "This place okay with you guys?"

We both nod. It's not like we'd turn down free food.

Still, as Connor orders, I feel uncomfortable. And I can tell from the way Joey keeps shifting that he does too. We don't get offered stuff like this a lot. Actually, I think Henry was the only one who did this. Usually after a good haul.

Connor lets us eat in the car. He even buys a beef patty for Roswell to eat. He doesn't mind that our dog sits between us on the seat. He says it's okay if we get something on the floor or seats, but neither one of us does. I can't remember the last time I saw Joey being so careful with his food.

When we're done, Joey clears his throat, then asks abruptly, "Is something wrong?"

I watch Connor frown in the rearview mirror. "Why would you ask that?"

"Because you're being really nice to us."

"Oh." Connor's frown deepens. "No, no there's nothing wrong."

I don't believe him. Neither does Joey. People aren't nice to us like this for no reason. Not adults anyway. Even Calum, who was really nice to me at the diner ended up using me. Oh, jeez, Calum. What he put up on his blog is totally false. I'm not from aliens. It was a coincidence that Joey and I were left in that field, and later got scars that matched the field almost exactly.

"I grew up in the system too," Connor says when we're quiet for a few minutes. "I ran away too. I was picked up and brought back more times than I could count."

"Did you ever have a family?" I ask.

"Yeah. When I was fourteen, I got adopted by a family I'd been staying with for about a year."

"If you got out of it, why'd you get a job doing something like this?" Joey asks. There's confusion in his voice, and maybe a little bit of irritation.

Connor shrugs. "Because I care. And I'm not blind. Lots of kids get placed with great families, but the system also lets kids fall through the cracks all the time. I can't help all of you, but I can help some."

"Have you worked with Camilla before?" I ask. We've been with her for as long as I can remember. I'd think we would've at least met Connor by now.

"No. Just transferred to the Payson office, actually. I go where I'm needed."

He speaks with an ease that lets me know he's telling the truth. He makes the job sound kind of appealing. Could I do this kind of thing when I'm older? I'm not sure I could hand kids off to foster families, hoping they'll be taken care of. I think I'd end up trying to foster every child that I ever worked with.

Joey must be reading my mind again, because he looks over at me suddenly and grins. Guess I'm not the only one who'd want to take every foster kid home.

So I ask Connor, "How do you just drop kids off at these places?"

Connor chuckles, switches lanes to pass a slow-moving RV, then gets back in the same lane. "It's not easy, I'll tell you that. Some of the doorsteps I was dumped on, the houses were rough. All I can do is try my best to make sure the kids I send off are getting treated well. But it's hard to leave them, even when I know the home is a good one. Because I'm still just another person that leaves them, you know?"

Joey and I both nod at the same time. We know probably better than most.

"So, you're working with Camilla now?" Joey asks, his voice tentative.

"Yep."

"Do you think . . . there's any way Jordie and I could get placed in a home together again?"

"Well, Camilla's actually looking into a home right now that's willing to take you both."

My heart jumps even as I try to squash it back down. "Really?"

"Yeah. But nothing's set in stone yet, okay?"

"We know," Joey answers. But I can see the hope in his eyes too, feel it radiating off him. If Camilla found one more family to take us in together, then maybe she'll be able to find more. Maybe we won't have to be split up, but I don't feel super hopeful. Even if we do get split up, I'm sure we'd be able to see each other on weekends or something. And Payson's pretty small, so we could even end up at the same schools. But it wouldn't be the same. I'd miss talking to him late at night when I can't sleep or listening to the sound of his even breathing when he drifts off. I'd miss watching him get money from doing outrageous dares. I'd miss him looking out for me.

And I think I'd always worry that maybe he ended up with

another guy like the one who would kick Rocky. Or even worse, the foster mom who burned us. How could I possibly sleep or eat or breathe if Joey was in a place like that without me?

The thought makes me sick to my stomach, and I start taking deep breaths so I don't see my burger and fries again. This new foster family has to work out. They have to take us and keep us, at least long enough for another family to decide they're okay with taking in twins who've gotten into a little bit of trouble.

Wordlessly, Joey reaches over Roswell's body and squeezes my hand.

As we're taking the exit back into Payson, Connor's phone rings in the console. Carefully, he steers the car to the shoulder of the road before answering his phone. Then he's silent for a long time. There's a woman's voice on the other end. I'm pretty sure it's Camilla.

"Really?" Connor asks after a long period of silence on his end.

The voice answers back, then Connor ends the call. "Good news, boys. That was Camilla. She said the person willing to take you in cleared the checks. When we get back to Payson, I'll take you straight to the office."

"We get to stay together?" Joey asks. His voice sounds small and almost afraid. Roswell shifts closer to him and licks his hand.

My brother smiles, his shoulders relaxing a little as he reaches to pet our dog.

"Yep." Connor's smiling wide.

"What's going to happen to Roswell?" I ask. "Our dog. Can we keep him?"

"I . . . don't know. You'll have to talk to your new foster parent about that."

"Have you met them?" I ask. "The couple that's taking us in?"

"Only briefly. And it's a guy, not a couple."

Joey glances at me. A guy? We rarely get taken in by single guys. It's usually a couple or just a woman. Henry was the only single guy to take us in.

"You'll meet him soon enough," Connor says, turning onto Main Street. The sun's starting to come up, rising between the buildings. I'm so tired that I'm starting to feel sick. It happens when I don't get enough sleep for long periods of time.

I hope Camilla's already got all the paperwork and everything sorted because I'll be ready to collapse when we get to the new foster home.

Connor finally turns into the parking lot of the DSS office Joey and I have become so familiar with. I can't count the number of days we've spent here, waiting on word of what was going to happen to us next.

Once Connor parks the car, he gets out and opens the door for us again. "It's okay," he says when he sees me reaching for the bag of garbage from McDonald's. "Leave it for now. Let's get inside."

Joey and I follow him up the cement steps and into the short brick building. In a lot of ways, this place is as familiar to me as any foster home I've stayed at. Wanda's at the receptionist's desk, and she gives us a bright wave when we walk inside.

The American flag is still in the corner behind her, next to the Arizona state flag. There's a scorch mark on the floor in the doorway, where a power cord once blew. Joey and I were here when it happened. He screamed louder than I'd ever heard him.

In the lobby, there are several chairs, each one more uncomfortable than the last. I can't count the number of times I've fallen asleep here, hoping not to wake with a muscle spasm because of the cramped seating.

Connor leads us all the way to Camilla's desk. As soon as she sees us, she jumps from her seat and grabs us both in a hug. It feels weird. It's the first time she's ever done that.

"Thank God you're both okay," she says, pulling away so she can get a good look at us. Then she glances down at Roswell. "And who's this?"

"Roswell," I answer. "We found him."

Camilla smiles and releases us long enough to bend and pet Roswell's head. Then she straightens and fixes me with a concerned look. "The police officer who got in touch with me said you'd been hurt, Jordie."

"It was just my knees," I answer, trying to mask how tired I sound when I speak. "And they fixed them for me."

She squeezes my shoulder, then glances up at Connor. "Did you get them something to eat?"

"Yeah."

"Thank you so much for heading out so late to get them."

"Not a problem." He gives us both warm smiles. "I'm gonna take off. But if you two need me for anything, let Camilla know. She'll get in touch with me."

Joey and I thank him, then he turns and heads back the way we came.

"Okay," Camilla says, pulling out the two chairs across from her desk. More chairs I've become familiar with. "Sit. Tell me everything that happened since you left."

THIRTY-ONE

We tell Camilla everything. Joey even tells her about picking the lock on a vending machine to get money for our bus tickets after I let our stuff get stolen. It makes my ears burn when he brings that part of the story up.

When we get to the part about Area 51, Joey hesitates and looks over at me.

"If this is about the military base, the police chief already told me that you snuck onto it," Camilla says. Her gaze shifts to me. "I'm sorry you didn't find what you were looking for."

I shrug. In a way, I think I kind of did. In Nevada, I realized being with Joey was more important to me than ever finding our parents. And if we never find them, I'll find a way to live with that too.

Roswell sits at my feet the entire time, his ears perking up at the slightest sounds.

"I told him everything," Joey blurts. "About Melinda and what she did with the cigarette lighter."

There's guilt in his voice, and I want to reach out and touch him, let him know I'm okay, but I don't think he'd appreciate it in front of Camilla.

"I know we weren't supposed to, but we were on the base and the soldiers had guns on us and I wasn't sure what else to do."

"It's all right." Camilla holds her hands up to stop him. "Jordie was having dreams about it. His mind was already on its way to waking that up for him."

Joey nods, but he still looks kind of miserable.

Camilla glances back at me. "How are you feeling about it?"

"I'm okay." I drop my gaze so I don't have to look in her eyes. "I feel really stupid that I forgot it."

"You didn't forget it," she says. "Your mind just blocked it to protect you. It was doing what it was supposed to do."

"But Joey didn't have to block it."

"Everyone's mind is different." Her voice is soft, trying to sooth. "Lots of kids repress traumatic experiences. There's nothing wrong with you."

I stay silent, not really sure how I should respond. It doesn't matter that lots of kids do it. I bet they didn't lead their brother and friend on some wild goose chase across three states only to wind up exactly where they started.

"So, Connor told us that you found someone who's willing to take us in together," Joey prompts. "A guy. Is that true?"

"Yes." Her voice is higher now, excited. "He's been cleared for fostering kids, and the agent who handled his application spoke very highly of him. But there is a slight difference between him and the other homes you've lived in. You'd be going to New Mexico."

Thirty-two

Leaving Arizona? I'm not really sure how I'm supposed to feel about that. Arizona has always been my home. And now it means leaving Nadia, the best friend we've ever had. But . . . "If it means Joey and I get to stay together, then I don't care where we have to move."

Her smile softens. "I thought you'd say that. The only other thing you two need to be aware of is that by moving to New Mexico, I would no longer be the social worker in charge of your case. You'll be assigned a new caseworker who's based in the area."

My heart sinks. Maybe Camilla wasn't there with us through everything, but she was *there*. We always knew that all we had to do was call her, and she would show up. "But what if we need you?"

She gives us another smile. "It's okay, guys. This is a good thing, you moving to a new place. I'll make sure you get a great social worker there, and you know you can always call me. Anytime."

Joey nods, but my stomach ties itself back into a knot. "I don't want a new social worker."

Her smile turns a little sad, and she lays her free hand on top of my head. I close my eyes at her touch, almost as familiar to me as Joey's is. "You guys are going to be okay. This is the way it's supposed to go. But I'll always be here if you need me."

"Okay." The word hurts coming out, even though I know she's right.

"Would you like to meet your new foster dad?"

"He's already here?" I ask. I'm used to waiting in the office while she talks with the new parents.

"Yes. He's been here for a while waiting for you two."

I glance at Joey, watch the doubt and confusion and fear swim in his eyes. "Yeah. Can we have just have a second first?"

"Sure." She stands. "But I'll be past the glass partition so I'll be able to see if you leave." She winks when she says it, but there's something in the lines of worry on her face that tells me she's not going to forget our disappearing act for a long time.

As soon as I'm sure Camilla's far enough away that she can't overhear us, I look back at Joey. "What do you think?"

"I don't know." He blows out a long breath. His voice is shaky. "It seems too good to be true."

"That she found someone willing to take us both?"

"No. That he wants us." He shakes his head. "Why on earth would someone from a completely different state care about two kids he's never even met?"

"I'd never thought of that." I pause, then realizing how stupid that sounds, I add, "Of course I spent the last five years thinking we were part of an alien race, so I guess it shouldn't really count."

He smiles. Just a little one. But at least it's a real one. Then he says softly, "I'm scared, Jordie."

"I know. I am too." Through my excitement, I feel the fear too. We *need* this to work.

Camilla reappears on the other side of the glass partition. "You boys ready?"

I look one more time at Joey, and he gives me a nod. So I stand, and he follows. Roswell pops up onto all fours and takes his spot between us, like a really mangy guardian angel.

Camilla gives him a smile. "He seems very fond of the two of you."

"He's a good dog," I say, reaching to rub his head. My hand is shaking. "Can we keep him?"

She gives the same answer Connor did. "You'll have to talk to your new foster dad about it."

Camilla leads us to the big conference room at the end of the hall. We almost never come in here. It's for big, important moments. And we haven't had any of those. I do remember playing in it a few times when Joey and I were really little, and Camilla was searching for a foster family for us.

She stops at the door and turns back to look at us. "If you boys need anything, at any time, even if it's just a five-minute break, all you have to do is say so, okay?"

We nod. Then she opens the door, and I get the first glimpse of our newest foster father.

His eyes are bright green. His hair is brown and a little long, close to his neck. He's dressed like us, in worn blue jeans and a T-shirt.

He also looks as tired as I feel. He has a ball cap in his hands that's obviously been twisted so many times in the past couple days that it won't ever straighten out again.

As soon as we step inside the room, he stops pacing and stares at us.

"Sam, this is Joey and Jordie." She puts a hand on our shoulders as she introduces us.

The man, Sam, stops twisting his hat immediately. "Hi, boys. It's nice to meet you."

"Why did you come all the way from New Mexico for us?" Joey asks, crossing his arms over his chest.

I expect Sam to get mad, maybe even Camilla, but neither one of them does.

Sam glances down at his twisted ball cap. "I grew up in the system too. I know what it can be like. When I saw you on the news, I just . . . I wanted to help. It's as simple as that."

I glance at Joey, but he's busy staring at the conference room table. I can feel the fear radiating off him, the same way I felt it when we were at Camilla's desk.

When we stay silent, Sam clears his throat. "Camilla told me the two of you have been through a lot of foster homes."

I still keep my mouth shut. I'm not really sure what to say to that. I don't want to talk about our homes, or the families that decided they didn't want us. That list isn't exactly a ringing endorsement for us.

Sam twists the hat tighter. "I was in seventeen before I aged out of the system. I was orphaned at four, though. I just . . . I'm sorry for all you've been through."

I swallow around the painful lump in my throat. I don't

really want him to feel sorry for us, but maybe that's just something people will always do.

Camilla gives me and Joey both a gentle poke in the back to get us to move farther into the conference room.

My legs shake as I take a step closer to Sam. "Where do you live?" I ask. My voice sounds rusty, like I haven't used it in days.

He looks at me, relief flashing in his eyes at the fact that I asked him a question. "Well, it's a tiny town in New Mexico, actually. Called Truth or Consequences."

Joey shoots him a suspicious look. "That's not a real place."

"It is." He pulls his phone out and taps at the screen before turning it to show us. He's right. It really does exist. It has a population of around five thousand.

"It's about an hour outside of Las Cruces," Sam says.

Joey glances at me. While we were passing through Las Cruces in search of a family, Sam was doing the same in the opposite direction.

"It's pretty small, but it's a great place to live." His words are nervous, like he's afraid we won't like it.

"Were you born there?" I ask.

"No. I was born in Oklahoma, actually." He smiles a little. "After college, I just picked the closest city that had a cool name and went with it." He shrugs. "You can make pretty weird decisions in your early twenties."

I've already made pretty weird decisions, and I'm only twelve.

"So what do you do? Like for a job?" Joey asks, inching just a little closer to Sam.

The move doesn't go unnoticed. Sam's eyes soften, and his smile widens a little. "Well, I work in construction, but I also just invested in a horse ranch. Truth or Consequences gets a lot of tourists, and most of them are big into riding. I'm hoping to have it up and running by next summer."

Joey likes the answer. He likes the idea of being on a ranch and around horses. I think he loves animals even more than I do.

I glance down at Roswell. "Can our dog come too?"

"Of course." He answers so quickly, like he's been waiting for us to ask for something he can actually give us.

Camilla touches our shoulders again. "If you two are okay here, I'm going to get the rest of the paperwork finalized."

We both nod. Sam does too. We all do it in varying degrees of uncertainty, but we nod. We're going to be living with him. We should be okay to stay in a room with him for a few minutes.

As soon as she's gone and the door has closed behind her, Sam lets out a slow, shaky breath. "Can we sit?"

Joey and I move immediately to the left side of the table. I take the chair closest to Sam, who sits at the head of the table. He puts his crushed ball cap on the dark wood and rubs his eyes. Up close, he looks even more tired than I thought he was when I first saw him.

"So . . . when'd you get here?" Joey asks.

"Two days ago. I was at my neighbor's house and I saw your pictures on the news." He shakes his head a little and smiles. "I knew as soon as I saw you. I've been preparing to foster for a while, home checks and classes and everything. I wanted to get the ranch done first, but I just couldn't not try for you two."

"You're really taking us to live with you?" I ask.

"Yeah. I mean, as soon as all the paperwork is signed and finalized. But we've already got approval."

Joey clears his throat suddenly and stands. "I have to go to the bathroom."

I look up at him, asking him silently if he wants me to come with him. Not to the bathroom, but just to talk. But he shakes his head slightly, then leaves the room, closing the door softly behind him.

Sam watches him go, his eyebrows drawn down in a frown. "I know you guys have been through a lot. It's okay if he's scared."

"Oh, I'm not sure Joey's scared of anything," I answer. "I've seen him do all kinds of stuff that lots of other people would be afraid of."

"Yeah?" He leans slightly forward in his chair. "Like what?"

"Um." I squirm, suddenly wondering if it's such a good idea to tell this guy we're about to go live with about all the stuff Joey's done that has gotten him into trouble. "Just stuff."

When he keeps watching me, waiting, I say, "It was nothing bad, the stuff he did. It was a lot of dares, really. Guys would bet him that he wouldn't do something, and he'd do it." I feel like I'm making him sound bad, so I add, "It's how he got me lunch money. Without him, I wouldn't have gotten to eat some days."

"Your foster families didn't make sure you guys got food?" There's no surprise in his voice. I'm guessing he's been there too.

"Some of them did. Some of them were really nice," I say, thinking of Henry and of Darla and Mitch. "And others . . . maybe not so much." I feel guilty saying that, like I'm saying Camilla wasn't good at finding us homes.

"You think we should check on your brother?" Sam asks. He's starting to twist his hat in his hands again. "He's been gone awhile."

"He'll come back when he's ready," I answer. I'm afraid if Joey's gone a long time, Sam will get mad at him. So I add, "He's really great, you know. He's awesome."

Sam's mouth curls into a smile. "Yeah? He seems a little shy."

I try to hide my own smile because Joey is the least shy person I've ever met. "You just have to get to know him."

Sam nods, and before the silence can start stretching too long again, I ask, "Do you have pictures of your ranch?"

"Oh yeah." He pulls his phone back out and taps the screen a couple times. Then he lays it on the wooden table and slides it carefully toward me. "That's the main house, where I live. A couple of my friends live with me there too, but there's plenty of room for you guys. They're helping me get it up and running."

I'll say. The sprawling house is huge. Way bigger than I thought he'd have. "Do you have a family? Like a wife or . . . other kids?"

"No wife, no kids," he answers. "I'm not sure marriage is in the cards for me, to be honest."

I stare down at the massive blue-and-white house. The evening sun is glinting off the windows. There's a small walkway that leads to the blue front door. There's a huge cement slab off to the side that ends at a three-car garage. A rusty red pickup truck is parked just in front of one of the doors.

He reaches over slowly, like he's afraid of scaring me. Then he uses his index finger to flip to the next picture. "These are the stables."

I smile as I look down at the stalls. They're all full of horses already. "How many do you have?"

"Horses? Eighteen."

Eighteen? That's more than I've seen in my life. "Have you named them?"

"Oh yeah, they all have names." He points to the first one and starts rattling off all eighteen names. Then he says he has a yellow lab named Trixie.

I smile at the picture of her. Joey and I have both always wanted a dog, and now we're going to have two.

"We can come back to visit Payson too," Sam says. "If you guys want."

I think about Nadia. It'll probably be a year before her dad even lets us near her again. "I'd like that."

The door opens behind us, and I turn as Joey steps into the room. He shuts the door softly, takes the seat next to me again. His eyes are rimmed with red.

Sam notices too. His mouth opens, but no sound comes out.

Joey clears his throat and glances at the phone. "Cool dog. Is she yours?"

Sam drops his gaze back to the phone with a nod. "She's four years old."

When Sam goes back to the beginning of the photos to show Joey the horses, I switch seats with my brother so he can have a better view. His back and shoulders are stiff; he's uncomfortable being around Sam.

He may not be from outer space, but Sam is still an alien to us.

Remembering to Forget Blog

Repressed memories, or "dissociative amnesia," is what occurs when you experience something so traumatic, your brain checks out and forces you to forget about what's happened. It's a survival technique, and it's very real.

Repressed memories are often related to childhood traumas, such as abuse, but they can occur in anyone. Adults can experience repressed memories when they've been through a traumatic event like a robbery, shooting, or having served in a war.

Most of the time, the memories begin to come back on their own, usually having been triggered by something that makes you remember.

If you are experiencing memories resurfacing, please reach out to a crisis counselor or licensed therapist for help.

THIRTY-THREE

When Camilla calls Sam out to her desk to get the rest of the paperwork signed, I lean back in my chair and stare up at the ceiling.

Joey knocks his knee into mine. "So what do you think of Sam?"

I turn my head to look at him, even though it makes my neck pinch. "He seems okay. Nice. I like his house."

"Same." He blows out a breath and runs his hands over a spot of dirt on the left leg of his shorts.

"Are you worried?" I ask.

"No." He hesitates for a long second, then says, "Well, maybe a little. It just seems . . ."

"Too good to be true?" I offer, even though I don't like saying it.

"Yeah," Joey says, looking away from me like he doesn't want to talk about it either. "It's just . . . we haven't exactly been lucky in the family department. What are the odds that we're really going to stay with him? That it'll be a good home?"

"I don't know," I answer truthfully.

"It'll be fine though," Joey says suddenly, bracingly. "We've been through plenty of homes so far. If this is another one that doesn't work out, it's no big deal."

It's so obviously a lie that all I can do is look at him.

Slowly, I start mentally flipping through all the homes we've been in for as long as I can remember. Some feel kind of new, since my memory's been a little hazy after Melinda's abuse. When her name enters my head, I can't help it. I lift my arm and feel the first burn closest to the base of my spine, under my T-shirt.

Joey watches me, his eyes clouded. "I'm sorry I didn't tell you about that before now."

I shrug even though it still hurts to think of him keeping it from me for so long. I'd thought we told each other everything. "They said not to tell me."

"I know." He scratches the back of his neck, creating angry white lines in the middle of a bright pink sunburn. "When they said we shouldn't tell you, I was really relieved."

"Why?"

"Seriously?" He rolls his eyes. "Because I didn't want you to have that in your head. It was better when you didn't remember."

"You don't know that." I sit up straight. "If I'd known, I wouldn't have dragged you all over the place looking for . . . aliens."

My cheeks heat when I use the word. I can't believe less than twenty-four hours ago, I truly thought maybe we were related to little green men that flew around in spaceships.

Joey knocks his knee into mine again. "Hey. Just because we're not related to them doesn't mean they don't exist. I believe Alvin. And even Beth to some extent. Besides, if we hadn't done that, our pictures never would've been in the news, and Sam wouldn't have known we were here."

That is a good point. Although still . . . "You should've made me stop, Joey. How could you let me do that?"

He shrugs. "I didn't know what else to do. I was worried if I asked Camilla for permission to tell you, she'd make us come home. Or worse, she'd tell us she was splitting us up. Jordie, I know I've done a lot of stupid things, and I've gotten hurt plenty of times because of it. But I couldn't let you go to a home without me. We weren't built to be apart. You know that. I felt like Roswell was the best option to keep us together."

At the sound of his name, Roswell perks up and rests his chin on my thigh, looking up at me with his dark, shiny eyes. I love that he's already responding to it.

Joey reaches over my lap to pet him. "Plus, if we hadn't gone, we wouldn't have him either. And he's worth the whole trip." He starts scratching behind Roswell's ears and uses the voice he reserves only for animals. "Who's a good boy? You are. Yes, you are."

"Joey."

He glances up at me, his hand still on Roswell's head. "Yeah?"

"Just don't lie to me anymore, okay? About important stuff."

He nods. "I won't."

I nod too.

"Jordie?"

"Yeah?"

"The time I kissed Carl wasn't on a dare. I just wanted to kiss him."

"I know."

He gives me a tentative smile that slowly widens. Then when his cheeks are pink, he turns to Roswell and goes back to petting him softly.

Thirty-four

When the door opens again, Camilla's the only one there. For a second, my heart drops when I think Sam must've left. He realized we weren't really what he wanted and doesn't want to try with us.

But Camilla's still smiling, so maybe it's okay.

She pulls out the chair across from us and sits. Then she places a handful of papers on the table. "All right, boys. I'm sorry this has taken so long, but we need to make sure everything's in order before we send you off."

Joey straightens but keeps his hand on Roswell's head. "Okay."

"I'm so happy Sam came here to find you guys." She's beaming. "I wanted to know if you had any questions at all."

"If Sam wants to keep us, then what'll happen if our birth parents suddenly get in touch?" Joey asks.

"Well, if we were to find them, they wouldn't just be given custody. They left you alone in a place where you could've died or been killed, so no one would just hand you over to them if they ever came looking for you."

The vise that's been on my heart since I learned the truth about how we wound up in the field loosens just a little. I didn't realize that was part of why I'd been in so much pain.

The thought of having to go live with the people who left us in a place like that on purpose was too hard.

I swallow as best I can with the massive lump in my throat. Sam traveled hundreds of miles to come get us, and our birth parents haven't once bothered to get in touch with us. "Do you think they're dead?"

Camilla's happy smile fades a little. "I don't know. To be honest, it's possible. It could be why no one's ever come forward to claim you two." She pushes the papers to the side, then reaches over to take my hand, and one of Joey's. She holds them tightly. "I'm so sorry that you almost had to be separated. I hope you both know I tried so hard to keep the two of you together."

"We know," I say. She looks so upset and guilty, like Joey did after he told me the truth about the scars on my back.

"We're really thankful for everything you've done," Joey says.

Camilla squeezes our hands, then releases them. "I'm going to get these scanned in, and then you guys will be free to go."

"Wait," I say as she starts to stand. When she looks back at me, I ask, "Do you remember that one home we were in? When we were moved out, we told you that the foster dad there was always kicking his dog. Do you know what happened to him?"

She frowns as she thinks back, but then her face clears. "Rocky. Of course I remember. We reported it to the ASPCA, and they placed the dog in another home."

I breathe out a sigh of relief as she stands. I can't believe she managed to get Rocky somewhere safe and away from that awful man.

As soon as the door closes behind her, I relax back into my chair and stare up at the ceiling. It's one of the ones that has a whole bunch of rectangles with lines between them. The lights are dim and humming just a little.

"What're you thinking?" I ask when Joey's been silent for a few minutes.

"It feels pretty surreal," he answers.

"Nadia taught you that word?"

"Shut up." He grins. Then he turns his head away from me and asks, "Are you scared?"

I sift through everything going on in my body and head, past all the happiness that Joey and I get to stay together. And underneath it is fear. The crippling kind. Because what if Sam turns out like some of our other foster parents?

"Yeah," I finally say. "Yeah, I'm scared."

Joey nods once. "Me too."

"What scares you the most?"

He's quiet for so long that I think maybe he won't answer me. Or maybe he'll lie and say he doesn't know, even though he just promised me he wouldn't lie to me anymore about the big stuff. But then he says, "I'm afraid I'll do something to get us kicked out. I know I was too much for some of the foster parents."

"Joey, that's not true." I think back to the way he called us garbage because we were left in a field. "We just weren't meant to be in those places, that's all. You didn't do anything to get us kicked out of any of them."

He turns his head to look at me. "What about Carl?"

JORDIE AND JOEY FELL FROM THE SKY

"Yeah, okay, you may have had something to do with that one, but it's not like it was right of him to kick us out because you and Carl kissed. It wasn't like it was a huge deal." Joey still doesn't look convinced, so I say, "Look, if you do something that gets us kicked out, I promise I won't hate you for it, okay?"

He studies my face, his eyebrows drawn down. Then he nods. "Yeah. Okay."

We fall into silence after that, and I spend the last few minutes in that room hoping that Sam doesn't turn out to be a bad guy. That he'll like us and won't care that Joey likes kissing boys. And that he'll be absolutely nothing like Melinda.

THIRTY-FIVE

Sam drives a blue four-door car. Joey and I take the back seat, even though there's an opening in the front next to Sam. Neither one of us is ready for that. I don't think Sam is either.

Sam starts the car and pulls out of the parking lot. "This isn't my car. I have a pickup back on the ranch. But it's not quite up for a long drive."

I look at Joey. We haven't been around cars that much, so I have no idea what's wrong with it enough for it to not be up for a long drive.

Sam keeps the radio turned off, so the silence just kind of fills up the car to the point that it feels suffocating. But I can't exactly ask him to start playing music. We won't be at that stage for a long time.

Instead, we sit with our hands in our laps, staring out the windows. We pass the school building Joey and I have been going to for the last year. There's the park we've gone to when our foster parents didn't want us in the house.

The grocery store we went to when Joey won money in a card game at school and we bought food. We pass Nadia's neighborhood, and I want to get out and tell her goodbye. But I don't think her parents would let me in the door.

We pass Katie's house.

And when Sam turns his blinker on to get onto the ramp

to take us to the exit, I look ahead at the field stretching out on my side of the car. "Wait."

Sam pulls the car to the side of the road, so quick that Joey jerks in his seat. "What? What is it? Is something wrong?"

"No," I tell Sam, unbuckling my seat belt. "It's just . . . Can I get out for a second?"

"Um . . ." He looks around, obviously caught between wanting to tell me no and not wanting to upset me. "Why?"

Joey looks from the window to me to Sam. "It's where they found us when we were babies. It's our field."

Understanding dawns in Sam's eyes, and it feels like permission, so I open the door and step out of the car. The heat from the midday sun hits my face, and I close my eyes against it, taking in a deep, steady breath.

When I hear Joey step out behind me, I head into the field. He follows at the same pace, and then in the distance, I hear another car door slam. Sam's coming in after us.

I make my way to the far left of the field. The crops have grown back since Joey and I were left here. There's no hint of the circle that flattened them twelve years ago.

The wind blows, bending the grass and stalks back. This is how it looked before Joey and I were left here. I don't think we'll ever really know what made the circle around us that day. We might never know how we ended up here.

Whatever the reason, I don't think Joey was right. We're not garbage. Maybe our parents just didn't love us at all. But maybe that's not our fault.

Joey moves up beside me, his arm pressed against mine. Together, we stare at the slowly moving crops, feel the sun beating down on the back of our necks.

Sam comes up behind us, breathing a little heavily. "This is where they found you?"

I nod. It's such a significant thing that I feel like I should remember when it actually happened, instead of only knowing about it from what people have told me.

Sam's quiet for a long, long minute. Then he says, "It's hard for me to imagine someone leaving anyone out here, let alone two babies."

"We're lucky the farmer found us when he did," Joey says, his voice soft. "You know, he wasn't even supposed to be in this part of the field that day? But something told him he should come out here. By the time they took us inside, they estimated we'd been out here about ten hours."

Sam lets out a cuss word, then gasps. "Don't repeat that."

It lightens the mood enough for me to smile. Joey's right, we were lucky. We didn't grow up with a family like everyone else I know, but we got the chance to grow up. Mr. Abrams found us in this field and he rescued us. Bouncing from home to home hasn't been easy, but at least we got to do it.

I want to go to his house, tell him how thankful I am that he found us and took care of us until social workers got there. But not right now. I'll send him a letter when I get to New Mexico. Right now, it's time for new beginnings.

THIRTY-SIX

It's a super long drive to Truth or Consequences. Actually, it's only about five hours, but after spending the last few days mainly on buses, it feels extra long.

Sam doesn't get mad when Joey and I fall asleep in the back seat. And he doesn't get mad when we have to stop right outside of the town because Roswell has to go to the bathroom.

When the town finally comes into view in the front windshield, Sam points to it. "That's home. It doesn't look like much, but I really think you two will like it here."

"Well. We saw pretty much all of what Payson had to offer, so I guess we can try this place," Joey says.

It makes Sam laugh. Joey's good at that. At making people smile even when they're sad or scared. He's done it for me so many times.

The tires crunch over the asphalt, then onto gravel when Sam pulls off the exit road that takes us into Truth or Consequences. I don't think I'll ever get tired of living in a place with that name. It's so much cooler than Payson.

In front of us, the blue sky stretches out forever, and it has three or four puffy white clouds in it.

Nerves flutter in my stomach as Sam drives us through the small town, past a pie shop that Sam tells us is only called the

Pie, even though that's not its full name. We go by the post office, a small grocery store, and a tiny bookstore.

"School is that way," Sam says, pointing out the window. "Close enough that I can drop you two off in the morning so you don't have to ride the bus. Unless you want to ride the bus, that's fine too. Whatever you want."

Sam talks quickly when he gets nervous. Less than twenty-four hours around him, and that's already become pretty clear. I like it. It's a good tell.

"I think we've had more than enough buses in our lives right now," Joey says, glancing at me.

I nod in agreement. Most of my muscles are still sore from sleeping in cramped positions.

"So you had your stuff stolen while you were on your trip?" Sam asks.

"Yes, sir," I answer. Joey and I didn't tell him the real reason behind our trip, even though we told Camilla. Neither one of us is ready, and I don't want him to think we're freaks this early on. Well, he'd think I was the freak, not Joey so much.

"Once you guys have had some sleep, we'll go into town and get you some things."

"You don't have to do that," I say at the same time Joey says, "We don't have any money yet."

Sam parks the car on the slab of concrete in front of the garage. "It's what dads do. I'm new at this too, so just let me do this, okay?"

Joey and I stay silent.

The seat creaks as Sam turns to face us. "My dad split before

I could walk. It was just me and my mom, and then it was just me. I know what it's like to not have a real home."

I watch his face, watch the truthfulness swim in his eyes. He actually means what he's saying.

"Okay," Joey finally says, then opens the door and scrambles out of the car. I follow him and take a deep breath of the fresh air.

Joey stares up at the sky, then squints as he looks out toward the horse stalls. "Can we see them?"

"In a bit. You guys should clean up and eat something first. You must be starving."

As if it was waiting for an invitation, my stomach starts growling. That meal from McDonald's that Connor bought us feels like it was three days ago.

Sam grins and jerks his head toward the main house. "Come on. There are some people I want you to meet."

Joey and I follow him up the worn wooden steps of the front porch. Near the door are three rocking chairs. One has a knitted blanket tossed over the back of it.

Sam opens the front door and steps inside.

Joey moves in front of me so I can follow him in. He did that at the other foster homes too, never trusting what was on the other side until he saw it for himself and decided it was okay if I came too.

I wait a few seconds, long enough for him to take a look around, then step in after him. The floors are wooden and creak just a little under my weight. There's a huge brown sofa against the far wall, with a large flat screen TV directly opposite it.

Past the living room is a hallway on one side, and three steps that lead into a kitchen. Pots clang from that direction, and then a woman fills the empty space above the three steps. "Sam? You're back? Thanks for calling."

She flips her bangs from her eyes and rushes down the steps. Her brown hair's pulled back into a high ponytail, but a few strands have fallen down around her face. She's dressed in blue jeans and a white T-shirt with a blue-and-black plaid shirt open over it.

Her smile is huge.

"Finally." She stops right in front of us, beaming.

"Anna, this is Joey, and this one's Jordie." He touches our shoulders when he says our names, just like Camilla did.

He gets us right. Lots of our foster parents couldn't tell us apart.

Before either one of us can speak, Anna wraps us both in a tight hug. She smells like cinnamon.

"Oh, I'm so glad you two are here," she says, pulling back to look at us. "When Sam called me, I almost didn't believe he'd actually gone through with it. I'm so glad he did. Just look at you two!"

Sam's grip on my shoulder tightens a little. He's nervous again. "Let them breathe, Anna. They need a little rest before dinner."

"I know, I know." She squeezes our shoulders, then leans up and kisses Sam's cheek. "Dinner will be ready in about an hour."

As soon as she disappears back into the kitchen, Sam lets out a breath.

"Is she your girlfriend?" Joey asks.

"Anna? No. She just works on the ranch. She was the first person I met when I moved here." He pats our shoulders. "Come on. I'll show you to your room."

We follow him down the long hallway. The floor is the same hardwood that's in the living room, but the walls here are white. And they're empty. In pretty much every foster home we've been in, there were pictures on the walls.

Sam stops at a wooden door and pushes it open. He stands off to the side, nervous again. "When I learned you guys were coming home with me, I got Anna and Bruce to go to Walmart and pick up a couple beds for you. I have another room, but it kind of serves as the attic right now. It's unfinished. But I can clean it out and you guys can have your own spaces."

"No, this is okay," Joey says, answering for both of us. "We always share a room. We like it."

He nods and stands in the doorway as we look around the new space. The beds are twin-size, with heavy blue comforters stretched across both. There's a nightstand between them, with a small lamp sitting on it. It's similar to the room we had at Henry's, and even Darla and Mitch's. It's clean and makes it feel like Sam really wants us to be comfortable here.

Joey's already at the window, raising the blinds so he can look outside. We have a perfect view of the horse stalls. Beyond that is nothing but blue sky and wide, open space.

"Like I said, we'll go get you guys some clothes tomorrow. Or maybe later tonight if you feel up for it. And anything else you need." He's gripping the doorframe now that he's no longer holding on to us.

"Can Roswell stay in our room?" I ask, thinking back to the bed I saw for Trixie in the living room.

"Yes, of course he can." He looks relieved that he has something he can give to us immediately, the same way he looked back in Payson, when I asked if Roswell could come with us.

Sensing he's allowed to stay, Roswell circles the room then curls up at the foot of a bed. I guess that one will be mine.

"Okay." Sam takes a step back. "Okay. You two get cleaned up. The bathroom's across the hall. And . . . and then I'll come get you for dinner."

Joey and I both nod, but neither one of us really breathes until Sam steps outside and shuts the door after himself. I wait a beat, listening to see if he'll lock us in here the same way some foster parents did. But it doesn't come. Instead, I listen to the sound of his footsteps retreating from the door.

Joey lets out a long breath and flops back on the bed closest to the window. He holds a hand up to his mouth, stifling a yawn. "How mad do you think he'd get if we didn't get cleaned up and we napped for an hour instead?"

"He'd probably think we were in kindergarten if we took a nap."

He grins, even though he's exhausted. His eyes are dim, but there's still excitement in them. Cautious excitement. Like me, he knows there could still be a chance this isn't our permanent home.

"I really don't think we should disobey him this early," I

mumble, hoping it doesn't upset Joey to say it. He's not exactly great at following rules.

"Okay." Joey shrugs, but doesn't move from the bed. "You go first though. And wake me if I'm asleep when you get back."

I do what he says, leaving our room to go to the bathroom. It's similar to the living room, with the same wooden floors. The walls in here are painted a light blue, and there's a window over the shower and tub, too high for anyone to see in. Hopefully.

I take a shower, and then have to put my same clothes back on. They're pretty grimy from all the stuff I've done the last few days. I have to pull the large Band-Aids off my knees because they get wet.

Underneath them, my skin is raw and red, and a little bit of blood leaks out from one of the cuts. I'll have to put another Band-Aid on if I don't want to get blood all over stuff.

I comb my fingers through my wet hair, then check the cabinet for Band-Aids, but there aren't any.

When I step out into the hallway, I can smell meat cooking, and hear Anna and Sam talking in the kitchen in low voices.

I cross the hallway and open the door to the bedroom again. I can't call it "my room" or "our room" yet. It always feels weird until we've lived in a place awhile. And even then, it's still weird. We've moved around so many places that nowhere feels like home.

But maybe this place can.

Joey's curled up on his bed, his mouth slightly open as he sleeps. I prod his shoulder to wake him. "Your turn."

He stumbles up from the bed and staggers out of the room.

The bathroom door clicks shut behind him, then I hear the water turn on.

I glance out the window once more, at freedom, then I take a breath and leave the room again. The hallway feels bigger walking down it alone than it felt when I was with Sam and Joey. The living room looks bigger too. I barely get to the end of the hallway before Roswell catches up to me. He nudges the back of my leg, right at my knee, as if he's asking why I would leave without him.

I scratch the top of his head in apology.

We cross the living room together, where he pauses to sniff out Trixie's bed. Then we take the three steps up and into the kitchen. It's bigger than any kitchen I've been in before, complete with a large island right in the center. It's where Anna's currently cutting some orange bell peppers.

Sam's across from her at the island, chopping red bell peppers, a lot slower than Anna. He pauses to drink from an open can of Coke when he sees me. "Hey, Jordie. You need something?"

"Um yeah." My cheeks heat, and I look away from him. "I was wondering if you had any Band-Aids. I got my other ones wet in the shower and I'm still bleeding a little."

"Yeah, sure." He stops chopping immediately and turns for the cabinet above the kitchen sink. When he opens it, he wraps his hand around a white box and pulls it down. "Come up here on the stool."

I do what he says. The stool's tall enough that I actually

have to use that little foothold bar at the bottom. My feet dangle about halfway down.

Sam opens the box on the counter and pulls out a tube of ointment, the same kind Officer Dean used on me back at the police station.

Sam kneels in front of me and frowns at the blood. "Anna? You think he should go in?"

Anna stops chopping and leans over the island to get a look. "For what? A Spider-Man Band-Aid and a lollipop? Treat his knee, Sam. That's not going to kill him."

Sam's ears turn red the same way Joey's do when he's embarrassed. "You're right. Sorry."

He clears his throat as Anna goes back to chopping. He squeezes a little of the ointment onto a piece of gauze and rubs it gently into the cuts. He's as careful as Officer Dean was when he worked on it.

"So, where'd you get this?" Sam asks.

"Oh, I fell on the street. Right before I went to the police station." I swallow hard because my throat's starting to feel tight. I don't want to remember that night. I don't want to think about what Joey told me while we were stuck in Area 51. Mostly, I don't want to think about how I let him down.

"Hey." Sam clears his throat again and concentrates super hard on the Band-Aid he's sticking to my knee. "Listen, Camilla told me that some of the other homes you've been in were pretty rough."

I look away from him, turning my gaze out the window

to that blue sky. The sun's streaming in, and someone raised the pane, so I can smell the fresh air.

"Jordie." Sam touches my leg, right underneath the cut he just worked on. "I need you to know that nothing like that will ever happen to you here, okay? We'll never hurt you."

I nod without taking my eyes off the window. No one's ever said that to me before. I want to blindly believe him, but Joey would tell me that's naive. But it's not Joey's voice in my head this time, telling me to be careful. It's my own voice.

I remember Rocky and the foster dad who would kick him. I knew we didn't always have the best homes, but after remembering our time with Melinda, I feel different. My mind knew I was able to handle the memory, and that means I'm strong. It's okay to listen to my own voice now.

Warden's Ranch Website

Ranches that cater mostly to tourists are called "guest ranches." They're also known as "dude ranches." Guest ranches are very popular tourist destinations, especially in western America. They allow for people to experience a taste of the "wild West" without any of the dangers of that nostalgic time.

The biggest activity on guest ranches is, without a doubt, horseback riding. Whether you're a first-time rider or a lifelong one, you'll be able to find a riding activity to participate in. Here at Warden's Ranch, you can participate in overnight pack trips, hunting trips, all-day rides, breakfast or lunch rides, nature rides, mountain rides, and a variety of daily trail rides.

We also have plenty of activities for children. Some are supervised, such as riding, while others are unsupervised. Check the appropriate level of supervision your child will need while participating.

THIRTY-SEVEN

When we get back from shopping for clothes, I'm pretty exhausted. But Sam mentions going out to check on the horses, and I don't want to miss out on that. Even though I know we'll have the option of seeing them tomorrow.

Sam walks between us on the way to the stalls, pointing out places on the ranch that we need to remember. Like the guesthouse, where the ranch hands live, and what areas to stay away from because there are too many snakes.

"Eventually, I'll show you around the trails," Sam says. "I want you guys to be familiar with them so when tourist season comes in a few months, you won't feel too overwhelmed. It'll be my first time actually running a ranch, so I've still got a lot to do."

I have a feeling we're going to be overwhelmed anyway, but I choose to keep my mouth shut about that.

When we reach the stalls, Sam ducks inside and stops at the first horse. "This is Pepper. He's my best one with kids. He's very gentle and great at sensing what you need before you have to indicate it to him."

He moves to the next horse, then the next, introducing them all to us. Occasionally he stops to add more hay to a stall, or to pet them if they're restless.

"Are all of these going to be guest horses?" I ask. "Are any of them just yours?"

He winks at me and beckons with his index finger to follow him. He leads us around the stalls and to a smaller structure, where six horses are stalled. "This one's mine. Her name's Starlight. Beautiful, isn't she?"

I gaze up at the brown horse, at the white star in the center of her forehead. Her coat looks so soft. I can't help but reach out to touch her, but before I make contact, I jerk my hand back. Then look at Sam for permission.

"It's okay," he says with a nod. "Go ahead."

I reach out again, resting my hand on her muzzle. She sniffs at my hand expectantly, making Sam laugh. He reaches into a bag hanging high on the wall and hands me a sugar cube. "Give her this. She'll love you."

I do as he says, and Starlight makes a contented sound.

"Do you take care of all of them by yourself?"

"Oh, no. Not even close. Bruce is the one in charge of this part of the ranch. And he's got a guy under him—Aaron—but he's off for the next two weeks. He and his husband just got married."

I glance at Joey to see his reaction to Sam's words. But I don't even have to look at his face because I feel relief flooding my limbs. If Sam's okay with a guy who likes other guys working for him, then maybe the fact that Joey likes boys won't bother him.

"This one's Anna's." Sam continues to a white horse with a pale gray mane. "Her name's Kala."

Then he shows us the last four in the stalls. "You guys can pick one for your own. I'll teach you how to ride."

"Seriously?" The word is out of my mouth before I can slow it down. I've never had a horse before—or any animal really. Now I'll have Roswell and a horse.

"Yeah." Sam gives me a gentle smile. "You really can't live on a ranch and not know how to ride."

I stop in front of one. Sam had called him Jasper. He's ghostly white, even whiter than Kala. He has brown spots on his chest. And the minute I reach out to him, he nuzzles my hand immediately. He's not even looking for a sugar cube. I can tell from how many cubes I've given out so far tonight.

"Jasper, huh?" Sam smiles. "That's a great choice. He's quiet but very playful. You'll love him."

Joey glances at all the horses, but his gaze keeps straying to the back of the stalls, where there's a big wooden fence set up, and a black horse running along the line of it.

With one more glance at Sam, who's busy petting Kala, Joey disappears out the back of the building.

Sam straightens. "What about you, Joey?"

I swallow and take my hand off Jasper's muzzle. "He, um, went outside. You didn't say we couldn't."

As soon as I say that last part, I feel stupid. But Sam doesn't comment on it. Instead, he turns and hurries out of the building, so I follow.

"Joey," he calls when he sees my brother leaning over the wooden fence. "No, don't go near that one. He's not trained or anything."

Joey barely acknowledges him. The horse is slowing to a trot as he approaches Joey. He stops in front of Joey and rears up on his back legs.

Sam lets out a swear word I'm sure I wasn't supposed to hear, and starts for my brother. The fear in Sam's movements makes me a little afraid, even though I've never been scared of horses. Or any animal.

But when we're a few steps from him, Joey reaches out and places a hand on the horse's muzzle. He bucks his head and brushes Joey off at first, but Joey does it again. Firmer this time.

The horse shuffles again, but stays still under my brother's hand. He even dips his head a little, pressing further into Joey's touch.

Sam reaches his side. "Joey, we haven't broken in this one yet, and I'm not sure we will. He's really wild."

"That's okay," Joey says. "I'm a little wild."

His certainty makes the knot in my stomach lessen.

Sam laughs, but it's winded and still scared. "You should choose one from the stalls."

"I want this one," Joey answers. "What's his name?"

Sam lets out a breath, like he's not sure he should tell him. But then he says softly, "Bandit."

Joey nods. "Perfect."

Sam pulls his shoulders back. He wants to argue with Joey, tell him he can't have Bandit. But even in the fading light of the evening, I can see the indecision on his face.

Joey glances back at him. "I promise not to ride him unless you or Anna is there."

Sam lets out a slow breath, then gives in with a nod.

My brother grins and gives Bandit one last pat before letting go of him. As soon as Joey backs off, Bandit returns to tearing up the fenced-in area, galloping back and forth.

Sam relaxes a little once Joey's fully away from the horse.

It might be mean to think, but I like that Sam's worried about Joey, that's he's concerned about him getting hurt. Because my brother *is* a little wild, and usually I'm the only one in his world who cares.

THIRTY-EIGHT

When we get back to the main house, I borrow the phone. Sam actually has one of those old on-the-wall phones that he still takes calls on. Joey and I go back to our room, and I dial Nadia's number.

She answers on the second ring, her voice just a whisper. "Hello?"

"Nadia? It's me, Jordie."

"Hang on," she whispers. I hear something click in the background, then the sound of a sprinkler. When she speaks again, her voice is almost at a normal volume. "Okay. How are you guys?"

"We're doing okay," I answer, glancing up to watch Joey confirm with a nod. "What about you? Were you in a lot of trouble?"

"Meh. Papa made me plead my case to an actual judge, and he was the prosecutor. The jury did not vote in my favor." She sighs. "It still could have been worse though. But tell me about your new foster dad. Is he nice?"

"Yeah. Really nice." I press my thumb into my thigh. "I mean, he seems like it."

"Dad told me that you guys were in New Mexico now. Is that true? What's it like there?"

"Hot." I roll my shoulders, feel the sunburn on my neck

stretch and pull. "But he lives on a really cool ranch. He has eighteen horses."

Nadia keeps peppering me with questions, and after a while, Joey falls asleep on his bed, so I get up and go into the living room so I don't wake him.

I sit in the dark on the couch, trying to keep my voice low so no one can hear me. Sam doesn't seem like the type to care about that kind of thing, but like I told Nadia, I barely know him. I remember Melinda seemed nice when we met her too.

By the time I hang up with Nadia, I'm so tired that I lie down on the couch instead of going back to the room I share with Joey. I lean over and set the phone on the coffee table, then ease back into the cushions. I'm sure I'll wake up at some point and stumble back into the room. But for now, I close my eyes and drift off to sleep, the image of Jasper still in my mind.

My skin is on fire. I'm crying because it hurts so bad. Joey's tugging on Melinda's arm, begging her to stop. I can feel each individual circle up and down my spine. It's just another way Joey and I are identical.

Sirens are starting to get closer outside. Melinda's screaming at me. I can't hear what she says because Joey's too loud. My ears are all clogged from crying. But her eyes are wild and angry. She hates us.

She's going to kill us.

I reach for Joey even though it hurts my back to move. I want him away from her. She's poison . . .

The white light blinds me. I'm so hot all over. It feels like my skin is on fire. I raise my hands, trying to scratch it off.

"Shh." Someone leans over me, the head so large it blocks the bright light. "You're okay, Jordie."

I close my eyes again because even with her blocking out the light, it still hurts to look at it. Everything hurts. "Mom?"

The woman squeezes my hand in response.

"We have to get them out of here," she says, her voice full of command and urgency.

I try to open my eyes, to get a better look at her, but the lights are starting to spin in a circle. They're different colors now, blue and green. The floor's moving.

Long, rubbery fingers grip my wrist.

"We have to send him now," the woman says. "He needs to go."

"I know it hurts," Joey says. "But you have to let them treat it or it'll hurt forever, okay?"

I nod even though I want to shake my head. How does it not hurt for Joey? How can he sit still while they touch the burns?

"I'll be here," Joey says. "I won't leave. And as soon as they're done, you can go back to sleep."

I take a breath and let it out slowly, trying to calm myself. I tried to teach Joey the trick, but he wasn't interested.

"He doesn't remember," Joey says. His voice is tight and pained. "He doesn't remember anything about what happened with Melinda. And he doesn't remember anything before that either."

"It was traumatic," a doctor in a white lab coat says. "His brain is trying to protect him by forcing him to block it."

"It happened to me too," Joey says. "Why won't I forget it? Why is it just him? Is something wrong with him?"

I keep my eyes closed in the hospital bed. I think it would take too much energy to open them. And I don't want to be part of this conversation.

The doctor's voice softens. "No, Joey, your brother's fine. It's a defense mechanism. Most likely one day he'll remember what happened."

"What should we do in the meantime?" Camilla asks. She's playing with the gold cross she always wears around her neck. "Should we try to tell him?"

"No, no. It'd be best for him if he remembered on his own. He'll be able to come to terms with it easier if he remembers instead of being told about it."

Joey's staring at Camilla, like he's silently asking if she agrees with what the doctor's saying.

She gives him a nod. She's shaking and her face is pale white. The call about us scared her. *We* scared her. I wonder if we've caused so much trouble that she'll hand us over to another social worker. But that's not really Camilla's style. She doesn't give up.

"He could've died," Joey mumbles. He's crying. I don't think I've seen Joey cry ever.

"I know." Camilla releases her necklace so she can reach

out and hug my brother. "I know, but he's okay. He'll be fine. You both will."

I open my mouth to call for Joey, let him know I'm okay, but the pain in my back is too bad. My vision blurs, and then there's nothing but blackness.

THIRTY-NINE

I bolt upright, trying to suck air into lungs that feel like they don't want to work anymore. My fingers are aching from where I have them clutching a chunky black afghan. For a second, I think I'm back at the hospital. But the sterile smell isn't here. Instead, it's earthy and clean in a good way.

And then I register the hand on my back, between my shoulder blades, supporting me as I try to orient myself.

"It's okay, Jordie." Sam's soft voice fills the big space. "It's just a nightmare. You're safe."

I pull in another breath, and then another. My heart doesn't want to calm down. My palms are sweaty, and my skin feels too hot. That dream was way worse than those memories I had on the bus rides while we were traveling. It was the same situation, but completely different. I didn't really remember the pain or the fear. I was too focused on all the things that were supposed to help me find our family.

Sam rubs my back carefully, like he's afraid of hurting me. I'm sure he can feel the raised scars up my spine underneath my thin T-shirt. "It's okay," he repeats. "You're not with them anymore."

I nod to show him I'm listening. I'm still sweaty and shaky, but the fear's starting to leave me. He's right; I am safe. Melinda's not with me anymore, and the pain in my back isn't real.

"Sorry," I finally say. My throat is raw and dry. "I didn't mean to wake you."

He chuckles, but it's a little forced. "This is my normal time to get up, kid."

I look up, checking out the still-dark living room. "What time is it?"

"About five."

Oh, jeez. Joey's never going to make it here.

"So what were you dreaming about?" Sam asks.

I glance over at him. He's kneeling on the floor right beside the couch. Already dressed in blue jeans and a white T-shirt.

"The day I got these." I motion toward my back, hoping he doesn't ask to see them.

"You want to tell me about it?"

I shake my head. I don't think talking about it will make me feel better. And besides, I don't want Sam hearing that stuff come out of my mouth yet. I know Camilla told him some of the homes were rough, but I don't think she told him everything.

"Okay." Sam moves his hand to my shoulder and gives it a quick squeeze. "Come on, can you get up? I want to show you something."

I throw the blankets off my legs, shivering in the cold air.

Sam grabs his jacket from the peg by the door and hands it to me. "Put your shoes on too."

I do what he says, taking some comfort in the familiarity of my worn sneakers on my feet. Then I follow him through the living room and out the front door.

When we step out onto the wooden porch, the planks creak

under our weight. Sam moves forward, resting his forearms on the porch railing. "Keep an eye on those rocks in the distance."

I move closer to him to get a better view. The sky's beginning to lighten, turning a pale blue. I stare at the pile of rocks far down the road. They jut up in different spots, giving it a weird, bumpy look.

Slowly, the sky starts turning pink. Then, through the gap in the rocks, I see the sun start to rise. It turns everything around us gold, makes the rocks look like they're sparkling.

"Pretty cool, huh?" Sam asks.

"It's amazing."

We watch the sun rise in silence, while I try to shake off the lingering fear from my nightmare. The sweat has cooled on my skin thanks to the fresh air. I almost wish I could stay here forever, in this spot. But Joey's not here, so it wouldn't feel right.

"I understand if you don't want to talk about it right now," Sam says, keeping his gaze fastened on the steadily rising sun. "But if you ever do, I'll be here, okay?"

"Okay." My voice sounds rusty, but Sam doesn't comment on it. He just reaches over and squeezes my shoulder gently.

"And it might be a good idea to set you up to talk to someone, when you're ready."

"You mean like a therapist?" I'd never considered something like that. I always had Joey to talk to.

"Yeah. Someone who's trained to deal with trauma. I saw one after a home I'd been in." His eyes darken slightly. "It's something I'd really like you to think about."

"Okay," I say again. Maybe it wouldn't be such a bad idea, especially if these nightmares keep going.

Joey stumbles out of the house behind us, rubbing sleep from his eyes. When he sees me, he throws me an accusatory glare.

"What?" I ask.

When Joey doesn't say anything, Sam releases my shoulder and takes a step back. "I'm gonna go get started on breakfast. Come in when you're ready. We have a lot of ground to cover today."

As soon as Sam disappears into the house, the screen door shutting softly behind him, Joey turns back to me with a frown. "Thanks for letting me know you were leaving the house."

"What? You wanted me to wake you up just to tell you I was stepping outside?" I regret the words a little, even as I say them. He's just looking out for me. It's what he's been doing practically since we were born. And he's taken it as his responsibility even more than I ever realized.

"Sorry," I say, gripping the railing of the porch. It's still cold from the night air, not warmed up by the sun yet. "I didn't think about it."

He grunts, his way of accepting the apology. He joins me at the edge of the porch, hands stuck in the pockets of his jeans. His T-shirt's rumpled and askew. He doesn't even have shoes on. Because he rushed out of the house to make sure I was okay.

"It's nice here," Joey says. He's staring at the sunrise, his eyebrows pulled down as he squints against the light.

"It is."

"Are you disappointed?" Joey asks. His voice is soft, telling me that whatever I say will stay between us.

"No." The truth is, I hadn't given much thought about having a human parent, because I was so certain ours were aliens. "I feel the same way here that I felt whenever I imagined living with the . . . others."

Joey glances at me. "And it's more convenient that he's a human, huh?"

I elbow his side. "Shut up."

He laughs and turns his head to face the sun again. "I think one day, we should keep going."

"What do you mean?"

"Go look for them again, the aliens. We saw a lot of the stuff on the trip, and even when we were babies and in the crop circles, that wasn't explained. It'd be kind of cool to go see what else is out there someday."

I try to hide my smile. Joey had been so full of disbelief about aliens when we first started this. "Yeah, one day. I'd like that."

He nods like it's settled.

"Thanks for coming with me to Roswell," I say. "And for going to Area 51. Even though you knew that what I was hoping for was impossible."

"I'm glad you know," Joey says. "I mean, I don't really want that stuff in your head like it's in mine, but it was really hard to not talk to you about it. We talk about everything."

"Except Carl," I say.

It's his turn to elbow me. "You shut up." He clears his throat. "I mean it, though. I didn't like keeping it from you."

"I'm sorry I wasn't there for you to talk to about it." I think of how Sam woke me, calmed me down after I had a nightmare about Melinda. I remember a few years ago, Joey was having a lot of nightmares, sometimes loud enough to wake our foster parents. That must've been what he was dreaming about.

Joey waves a hand like it's no big deal, but it is to me. He's always been there for me, and I want to be able to do the same for him. That's what family does.

But I get the feeling Joey wants it behind us for now. So I glance at the horses' stalls. "You're really taking Bandit?"

"Oh yeah. He reminds you of me, doesn't he?"

I shake my head, but tell him the truth. "Yeah, he does."

The smile slips off Joey's face, and he kicks at the porch with his bare toes. "Even if we stay permanently with Sam, you still need me, right?"

His voice is soft and quiet. He's scowling, like he hates himself for asking the question.

"What?" That thought had never even occurred to me. "You seriously think that if we ever found a permanent place, I wouldn't need you? Who's gonna teach me how to win at poker or do outrageous things for money? Or snore in the bed next to me, preventing me from sleeping?"

Joey laughs. "Okay, okay. I was just asking." He palms the back of his neck, like he's trying to rub out his embarrassment. Then he punches my shoulder and says he'll see me inside.

When he disappears back into the house, I take one more

look at the sun still rising high over the rocks. I take a deep breath, inhaling the cold air and the earthy smell of the ranch. I feel my crop circle scars shift and tighten when my muscles move.

I know they don't mean anything anymore, but they still signify where I came from. They don't mean I'm descended from aliens, but they are a mark of survival. And I think maybe that's even better.

Author's Note and Resources

Child abuse is a real issue that impacts thousands of children each year. And you don't have to be in the foster system to be hurt by people who are supposed to take care of you. When you're in a situation like the one Jordie and Joey experienced, it's easy to think you're the only one in the universe going through it. But there are those of us who got help and made it to the other side.

If you're in a situation or a home like Jordie and Joey's, there are places and people that can help you. Teachers, doctors, and social workers are required by law to report suspected abuse. There are also several hotlines open 24/7 with people who can help you.

If you're being abused, or have been abused, you're not alone or invisible. For every one person who tries to dim your light, there's another one waiting to watch it shine.

Childhelp National Child Abuse Hotline
www.childhelp.org/hotline
Open 24/7

RAINN
www.rainn.org
Open 24/7

National Domestic Violence Hotline

www.thehotline.org

Open 24/7

Together We Rise

www.togetherwerise.org/about-us

Foster Club

www.fosterclub.com

National Runaway Safeline

www.1800runaway.org

LGBT National Help Center

www.glbthotline.org

Acknowledgments

Biggest thanks to Heather Cashman, who's been the best agent I ever could've asked for. All your support and unwavering belief made this possible. Thanks to Mari Kesselring, who's been an amazing editor. I've loved working with you both! Thanks for loving Jordie as much as I do!

Thanks to Emily Temple, Jackie Dever, and Briana Wagner for making Jordie shine. Massive thanks to illustrator Thomas Girard for the amazing cover! Thanks to the entire team at Jolly Fish Press for believing in me and Jordie.

I didn't have my CPs on this because we went straight out with it. But a huge thanks to Alexandria Rogers and Adam Schmitt, who inspired me to write middle grade and who encouraged me so much. And Danielle Thurby for being one of the best friends I've ever had. Thanks for the brainstorming, listening to me rant, and always being so incredibly supportive.

Thanks to my mom, who fostered in me a love of Roswell and spaceships. And to my sisters, for always being there when I wanted to blow off writing and play video games.

Thanks to my English 111 college professor who told me I needed to start writing for a living.

And thank you for allowing me and Jordie into your lives and onto your bookshelf.

About the Author

Judi Lauren has been reading since she could first hold a book. Following her passion for working with words, she became an assistant editor at Entangled Publishing, and is now an editor at Radish Fiction. When not editing, she writes books for kids and teens about family, friendship, and surviving impossible things.